"There is no way you can make me marry you, Adam," Shay said, her voice wavering.

"No? Suppose I take you to court, Shay? It should make for an interesting custody case—father fights the woman who duped him for their unborn child. And you needn't think that you'd automatically win because you are the mother. Those days are gone forever."

"Don't, Adam," Shay pleaded, her heart thundering in her ears. "Why are you making these threats? You don't really want to marry me, you don't want the baby."

"I've always wanted children—that's the reason my first marriage fell apart. I wanted a family, and she didn't." He spoke quietly, sincerely, as Shay listened, anger turning to shock.

"Don't try to be noble, Adam. Don't pretend that you give a damn about me. You never once called me in the past two months—"

"Stop it, Shay. There's nothing you can say now to change my mind. I'm going to marry you." Suddenly he pulled her against him, bringing his mouth to hers, whispering promises to kiss all the hurt away. . . .

WHAT ARE *LOVESWEPT* ROMANCES?

They are stories of true romance and touching emotion. We believe those two very important ingredients are constants in our highly sensual and very believable stories in the *LOVESWEPT* line. Our goal is to give you, the reader, stories of consistently high quality that may sometimes make you laugh, sometimes make you cry, but are always fresh and creative and contain many delightful surprises within their pages.

Most romance fans read an enormous number of books. Those they truly love, they keep. Others may be traded with friends and soon forgotten. We hope that each *LOVESWEPT* romance will be a treasure—a "keeper." We will always try to publish

LOVE STORIES YOU'LL NEVER FORGET
BY AUTHORS YOU'LL ALWAYS REMEMBER

The Editors

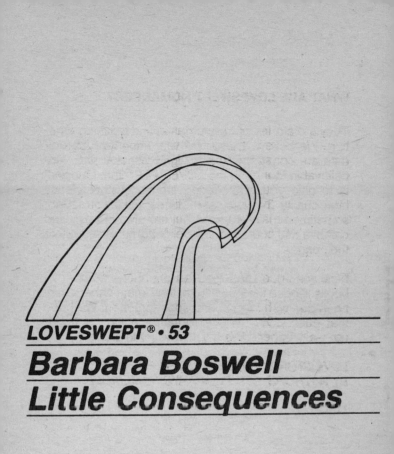

LOVESWEPT® • 53

Barbara Boswell
Little Consequences

BANTAM BOOKS • NEW YORK • TORONTO • LONDON • SYDNEY

LITTLE CONSEQUENCES

A Bantam Book / July 1984
Silver Signature edition / July 1991

If you would be interested in receiving protective vinyl
covers for your Loveswept books, please write to this
address for information:

Loveswept
Bantam Books
P.O. Box 985
Hicksville, NY 11802

ISBN 0-553-21654-6

Published simultaneously in the
United States and Canada

PRINTED IN THE UNITED STATES OF AMERICA

O   0 9 8 7 6 5 4 3 2

One

"More wine, Adam?" Shay didn't wait for his answer as she rose from her chair. Wine bottle in one hand, she leaned over him, laying her other hand on his shoulder, and refilled his glass. "It's very good, an excellent vintage, don't you think?" She leaned closer and carefully brushed the tips of her breasts against the solid muscles of his upper arm.

Adam turned slightly and she smiled at him, a warm invitation glowing in her dark blue eyes. He cleared his throat and reached for the wineglass. "Yes, excellent."

She handed him the bottle, and he examined the label. "Ahh. A Bernkasteler Doktor, 1971. The finest vintage of the finest Moselle."

"I'm glad you're enjoying it. Catherine did tell me that you're something of a wine connoisseur." Shay sat back down in her chair at the opposite end of the small table. "I wanted to find something very special for you . . . tonight." She slipped off her high-heeled patent-leather sandal and stretched her leg under the table. Her foot found his left ankle and gently stroked it before slipping under the cuff of his trousers to continue the sensuous massage. Her blue eyes never left his face.

Adam abruptly drained the contents of his glass. "What did you say the, er"—he shifted in his chair, drawing his legs under it—"name of the wine store was?" His breathing seemed to be growing more shallow.

Shay's foot followed his legs' withdrawal, again finding its target with unerring accuracy. "I don't believe I mentioned it." She moistened her lips with the tip of her tongue in a deliberately provocative gesture. "But if you're interested, it was Harry's, in downtown D.C."

"Of course, Harry's. I've been there many times myself. I believe it's the finest wine store in the area. Has Harry ever shown you his special—"

"Adam, will you dance with me?" Shay interrupted, her smile warm, seductive. The softly romantic strains of Johnny Mathis had been playing all through dinner and were, Shay hoped, a guaranteed turn-on. She'd once heard her brother, Case, tell one of his girlfriends that Johnny Mathis albums were the best make-out music of all time. Adam was thirty-six, only a few years younger than Case. Shay hoped he shared his generation's collective feelings about old Johnny.

Taking Adam's hand, Shay led him to the small open area in front of the rust-colored modular sofa. She moved into his arms with a small sigh, slowly winding her arms around his neck as she molded her body tightly against him. Her fingers played with the thick chestnut-brown hair at the collar of his starched yellow oxford cloth shirt, and she pressed her breasts into the solid wall of his chest. Slowly, sensuously, she moved her hips against his rock-hard thighs.

"Adam," she whispered, touching her lips to his neck. Her tongue traced an erotic pattern along his jawline. "Oh, Adam."

She felt his arms tightening around her, gathering

her closer, fitting her even more intimately against his unyielding masculine contours. It was the first move he had initiated, and a heady excitement surged through her. It was going to work! Until this moment she hadn't been sure, despite her carefully orchestrated plans.

All evening she had plied him with good food and wine, had smiled and flirted and given him every come-on sign she'd ever read about, only to have him react with polite reserve. For one heart-stopping moment, when he had begun to extol the virtues of Harry's wine cellar, she'd feared all was lost. An oenophile could discuss wine for hours. Her invitation to dance hadn't come a moment too soon.

And now . . . now she felt the hard, masculine response growing in him and she clung to him, moving in a sensual rhythm designed to excite him further. When she lifted her face expectantly, he didn't disappoint her. His mouth covered hers, and her lips parted instantly, pliantly, welcoming the thrust of his tongue into the warmly moist interior. His hands moved slowly down her back, his fingers tracing and kneading the length of her spine. The soft plum silk of her blouse felt sensuous and cool against her bare skin—she had, of course, deliberately omitted her bra—and Shay wondered if Adam was enjoying the tactile delights of the material too. Silk and velvet were two of the "Sensuous Fabrics" mentioned in the article in *Cosmopolitan*, "How to Seduce Him with Clothes." Shay had taken note and dressed accordingly. Her black velvet skirt was slit to the top of her thigh, another recommendation in the article.

She felt his hands slide over the softness of her skirt, over the firm curve of her buttocks, and heard his swift intake of breath. He had just discovered that she wasn't wearing any panties. It was time to make her move.

"Adam, I want you so." Her voice trembled as she fumbled with the buttons of his shirt. When her fingers encountered the soft, curly hair covering his chest, she felt a peculiar tightening in the pit of her stomach. Oh, dear heaven, it had to be tonight! "Please, Adam."

"I feel as if I've stepped into a fantasy," Adam murmured, his warm breath tickling her long neck.

Shay heard the humor in his voice and frowned. Humor played no part in a seduction scene, particularly one as crucial as this. She slipped her fingers beneath the waistband of his slacks, determined to set the scenario back on the right track. "It is a fantasy, Adam. And in fantasies anything that you want can happen." Her fingertips touched the bare skin of his stomach, and he jerked spasmodically. "It will happen, darling. Now."

She guided him into the small bedroom that was lit with two lilac-scented candles. Another tip from *Cosmo*. Johnny Mathis's soulful, longing voice filtered in from the living room. The colorful quilt on the bed was pulled back invitingly and soft pillows were stacked along the headboard. The sheets were several shades of her favorite color, purple, with tiny pink and white violets. It was a romantic setting gleaned from yet another magazine article, "The Sensuous Bedroom."

Shay cast a covert glance at Adam's face, but his expression was enigmatic. It was quite obvious that he was not bowled over with desire, as were the heroes in those paperback romances she had read— for research purposes, naturally. But he at least seemed willing enough. Willing and able? The thought struck her as funny, and she was hard-pressed not to laugh. That would never do. Adam might think she was laughing at him, and she dared not risk offending him. Not tonight, when he was so essential to her plans.

The next few moments were crucial, and it took every ounce of Shay's resolve to get through them. She unbuttoned her blouse slowly, her fingers unsteady. The silence was unnerving. Adam stood beside the bed, and she wished he would say something, anything, but he merely followed her every movement with cool gray eyes. It wasn't until she removed the pins from her hair and let the sable tresses fall over her shoulders that he uttered a sound. A murmur of surprise.

"It's so long." He reached out and touched a dark, silky strand. "Almost to your waist."

"I've never had it cut." Shay was proud of that. "Oh, I've trimmed the ends a little from time to time but—" She broke off, annoyed with herself. She was babbling. This was hardly the time or place to discuss hairstyles.

"You were wearing it up the night I met you at Catherine and Bill's party." Adam toyed with her hair, almost absently wrapping a long lock around his fingers.

"Yes," Shay whispered. Nervousness had begun to set in during the brief interruption. She willed him to make the next move, to do something, anything, to take the lead from her.

Adam continued to play idly with her hair. "How do you know the Benningtons?"

Shay's palms began to sweat. She didn't want him to question her too closely about the Benningtons, although it must be obvious to him that she was not in their usual circle of friends. "Through my brother."

She moved closer and started to loosen his tie. He had dressed formally for their date, wearing an expensive European-cut blue suit, a muted striped tie, and a Brooks Brothers shirt. His uniform, Shay thought with a flash of grim humor. This was the third time she had seen him, and his style of clothing hadn't varied. He dressed like the conservative, successful, and wealthy attorney that he was, like the blue-blooded scion he had always been.

Shay couldn't seem to undo the knot. She had never done this before, and felt a sudden urge to scream with impatience. She should have practiced with one of Case's ties.

"Who's your brother?"

Shay tried to conceal the irritation coursing through her. Adam was a typical lawyer, cross-examining her every statement. She endured enough of that from her sister, Candy. "My brother is Casey Flynn." She knew he wouldn't stop asking questions until he got an answer.

"Casey Flynn? The doctor at the Hospital Center's shock-trauma unit?" Adam seemed surprised. "Of course, Flynn. I didn't connect your name with his." He offered her no help with his tie, and Shay barely muffled a groan of frustration.

She decided to work on the buttons of his shirt. She'd had some luck with a few of them while they were dancing. But first his jacket had to go. "Flynn is a common name." She tugged the jacket off his shoulders and slipped it down his arms. "I wouldn't have expected you to make the connection."

"Catherine and Bill literally worship your brother. They fully credit him with saving little David's life two years ago after that terrible car accident."

"He did." Having completed unbuttoning his shirt, Shay decided to give the tie another try. This time she was successful and slid it from his neck. "Save David's life, that is. Case has saved hundreds of lives. He's probably the best trauma surgeon in Washington." She stood on tiptoe to slide the shirt from his shoulders. Then she carefully placed his jacket, tie, and shirt on the overstuffed armchair in the corner of the room. It was good etiquette to take proper care of a lover's clothes, so that he wouldn't have to leave looking like the unmade bed he'd just left. The direct quote from *Cosmopolitan*'s August issue had stuck in her mind as very good sense.

"But I think we've talked enough about Case and the Benningtons, Adam. I—" She swallowed hard. "I have more important things on my mind."

She removed her blouse and tossed it on the armchair's matching ottoman. She needn't take such care with her own clothes, since she wouldn't be leav-

ing the apartment immediately. She turned back to
Adam, fighting a nerve-shattering self-conscious-
ness. She had nothing to be ashamed of, she drilled
herself. She had a good body and should be proud of
it. Her breasts were full, firm, and high, her waist
small. Still her fingers were shaky as she unzipped
her skirt and slowly lowered it over the smooth curve
of her hips.

Something flickered in Adam's gunmetal gray eyes
and she saw a muscle clench convulsively in his jaw.
So he was not as cool as he appeared to be. Good!
Shay stepped out of her skirt, leaving it in a black velvet pool on the rug.

"Adam." She floated into his arms and heard him
groan as she nibbled delicately on a taut male nipple.

"God, Shay, what are you trying to do to me?" he
rasped out, running his fingers through her thick
mass of hair. His hand clenched the rounded softness of her buttocks as he arched her against him.

"Make love to me, Adam," she pleaded, burying her
face in the hair-roughened warmth of his chest. She
ran her hands over the muscles of his bare back, feeling his strength, his power. Her heart was pounding
wildly; her pulses were racing. All evening she had
remained detached, too concerned with arranging
the seduction to feel the sensations of an actual par-
ticipant. But now, as Adam's mouth claimed hers,
his tongue beginning an erotic exploration within, as
one of his large hands palmed her breast and teased
the nipple with his thumb, Shay felt a strange heat
course through her body.

His other hand kneaded the small of her back, then
moved lower, to the sensitive skin of her thighs. The
kiss deepened, demanding a response from her that
came naturally. Small whimpering sounds of pleasure escaped from her throat. When they descended
slowly, inevitably, to the bed, Shay wrapped herself
around him in hungry abandon. There was a deep
ache in her abdomen that radiated hotly to her lower
limbs, to the very core of her. He was so strong, so

warm. She wanted to be closer to him, to envelop him.

"Mmmm, you taste good. Like vintage Moselle wine." Adam's mouth hovered a few inches above her own as he lay beside her, his full six feet two inches stretched out on the bed. Shay, who had always considered herself tall at five six, felt petite next to him. It was an unfamiliar but pleasing sensation.

She smiled tremulously and reached up to trace his lips with her fingers. "You have wonderful features, Adam. It was one of the first things I noticed about you. Beautiful gray eyes with thick lashes, a good, straight nose, a strong jaw and chin." Her fingers traced each feature, as if committing them to memory. "A generous mouth and fine, straight teeth."

"Hey, I feel like I'm at a horse auction." Adam laughed, catching her hand to kiss her palm. "And I'm the horseflesh. But I'm glad you approve of my Wickwire heritage. Fine features, handed down from generation to generation."

He didn't know the half of it, Shay thought with an involuntary smile. He returned her smile, and for a moment their eyes met and held.

Adam drew a deep breath. "You're lovely, Shay. Beautiful."

"No, I'm not." She shook her head. "Oh, I'm passably good-looking, I guess," she said without false modesty, "but not the type you'd ever look at twice in a crowd. And I'm certainly far from beautiful."

Adam studied her face, the high cheekbones and wide-set dark blue eyes, the full mouth and firm but delicate chin. Perhaps she wasn't classically beautiful, but she was much more than passably good-looking. One didn't often see fair skin and blue eyes with such dark hair. The unusual combination was striking.

Still, she was right on target about his not looking at her twice in a crowded room. His eyes had flicked over her rather dismissingly the night of the Benningtons' party at their rambling home in the exclusive suburb of Potomac. He had made no attempt to approach her and introduce himself, until Catherine Bennington had taken a hand.

He remembered the moment well. Catherine had insisted that he come with her to the corner of the room where Shay stood alone, making no attempt to socialize with any of the other party guests. After introducing them, their hostess had not-so-discreetly slipped away, leaving the two in awkward silence. They had engaged in a few minutes of meaningless, strained small talk, then Shay surprised him with an invitation to dinner at her apartment the next week. He had accepted without enthusiasm, more out of deference to Catherine than to Shay. Catherine had made a point of introducing him to this girl; she obviously expected something to come out of it. And Catherine and Bill Bennington were good friends as well as clients.

Unfortunately, Shay Flynn wasn't his type. He'd known it at a glance. He preferred sophisticated women with polish and style, the products of prep schools and exclusive women's colleges. Conversely, he also liked women who were very beautiful and very brainless. Standing in the corner of the Benningtons' rambling home in her neat mauve shirt-dress and flat shoes, her hair pulled up into a prim knot, Shay Flynn had fit into neither category. He had braced himself for a dull evening and wryly debated charging his time to the Benningtons' account. The sexily dressed young woman who had opened the door this evening had stunned him, as had her subsequent behavior. Who would have ever guessed that she would come on to him like a hungry sex kitten? In heat!

"What are you thinking about, Adam?" Shay asked in a husky voice, trailing kisses from the curve of his shoulder to the hollow of his neck. Had he changed his mind? To have come so far and have him back out at the last minute . . . She couldn't let it happen! She might never work up the courage to try it again.

"You." Adam chuckled lazily as his hands roamed her body with leisurely exploring strokes. "And first impressions."

Shay felt a tremor of relief. "You make a marvelous first impression, Adam." She closed her eyes as his hand moved possessively along the inside of her thigh. Sharp needles of sexual excitement pricked every nerve, and she breathed deeply in an effort to gain control. "The first time I saw you, I—"

Her eyes flew open in alarm. As far as Adam knew, the first time she had seen him was last week at the Benningtons' party. He knew nothing of the research she had done, the days spent planning and checking . . .

"Yes?" Adam prompted. "The first time you saw me?"

Shay moved against him, entwining her limbs with his. It was definitely time to stop talking. "The first time I saw you I thought, 'What a smashing first impression that man makes.' "

"Brat." Adam gave her rump a playful swat. "So you aren't going to tell me?"

"We women are entitled to our little secrets." Shay reached for his belt buckle. "Aren't we?"

She heard Adam's sharp intake of breath as she slowly began to unzip his trousers, artfully brushing against him with her fingers. She was relieved when Adam finished what she had begun and removed the trousers himself. He tossed them carelessly to the floor, and, remembering the magazines' advice, Shay wondered if she should rush to hang them up. Instinct told her to remain where she was.

He wore blue cotton shorts, loose-fitting and similar in style to a pair of modestly cut swimming trunks. Shay was inordinately grateful. Had he sported colorful, sexy bikini underwear, she might have lost her nerve completely. She averted her eyes as he removed the remaining article and came to her.

"I want to please you, Adam," she whispered, quoting the heroine of a thrilling pirate saga she had found most erotic. She remembered every word in the passage and proceeded to say each one. "I want you to tell me what you want, for I want to be just what you want. I want you to possess me completely." To her delight, Adam reacted just as the lusty pirate had in that exciting tale.

He crushed her to him in a viselike grip. "Oh, God, Shay, what have you done to me? I want you so badly." He sounded as surprised as he felt. Shay was a tempting seductress, he thought dazedly as he pushed her deeper into the softness of the bed. She had taken him from bored disinterest to yearning passion in the course of a few hours.

They kissed deeply, intimately, until Shay's mind was spinning senselessly, deferring to the needs that Adam aroused within her. Her unexpectedly wild hunger astonished her. She'd never dreamed she would be swept along in the tide of passion she had managed to evoke in Adam.

"Your breasts are so lovely," Adam murmured huskily as his hands cupped and kneaded and caressed the sensitive ivory flesh. "So full and firm and lovely." He lowered his mouth to the taut pink crest and gently encircled it with his tongue. Shay moaned and writhed beneath him.

"You like having your nipples touched." Adam smiled his satisfaction. "Every time I touch you there, you whimper and squirm, as if you're begging for more." He took each nipple alternately in his mouth, teasing with his tongue, then nibbling sensuously with his teeth. When he began to suck gently, Shay thought she would lose her mind.

It wasn't supposed to happen this way, she thought dizzily, even as she clutched his head to her breast, demanding more. She was supposed to be the one in command. In her carefully formulated plan, Adam was supposed to lose all reason in the heat of physical sensation.

But his hands were caressing her with an expertise that made her senses reel. He seemed to know exactly where she wanted to be touched and how to touch her so that she was spinning out of control. She twisted restlessly beneath his fingers as they traced a tortuous, erotic pattern along the silky, soft skin of her inner thighs. Her legs shifted languidly in an unconscious feminine invitation, but he didn't accept the offer immediately. Instead his fingers continued to play over her hips and thighs, coming closer, closer to the heart of her passion, but never close enough. The teasing continued until Shay arched her hips toward his hand and uttered an incoherent plea.

"Poor baby," Adam soothed, dipping his tongue into her navel. "It's cruel of me to tease you, isn't it?" His mouth moved lower, and Shay stifled a small sob of desire. "But I wanted to take a little revenge for the way you've driven me mad tonight."

His mouth found the intimate warmth of her, and Shay clutched at him convulsively, suddenly terrified by the waves of passion surging through her. Every nerve seemed to have come alive with an excruciating awareness, every muscle was taut with the tightly coiled spiral of desire that threatened to explode within her. It was so wondrously pleasurable, this strange and unfamiliar ecstasy; one could easily become addicted to it, to want it over and over again. To want *him* over and over again, Shay amended wildly.

"Let yourself go, darling," Adam whispered encouragingly. "You're so very close, aren't you? Just let go and let me take care of you."

She couldn't give in to it, couldn't give in to him. She must fight to pull herself out of the swirling depths that threatened to engulf her. She had Adam Wickwire for a short time only. She must never forget that, must not let him trap her into needing him beyond the here and now.

"Adam, I—I—"

He took her in his arms then, stroking her with long, soothing caresses. "It's all right, sweet. You're really a little shy, aren't you?" He kissed her warmly, lingeringly. "Next time we'll get past those inhibitions, hmmm?"

Next time. The words swirled dizzily through her brain. Did that mean he wanted to stay with her? Her heart leaped with hopeful anticipation. She had worried about his leaving her immediately afterward, and wondered if she possessed sufficient allure to keep him for the rest of the weekend. It was vital that she do so.

"I want you, Shay." Adam touched her intimately, and she quivered. "And I can feel how much you want me. Are you ready for me, darling?" His voice was deep and husky in her ear.

"Yes, Adam," she whispered, and she began to tremble. It was time. It was finally going to happen. The first step of her most cherished dream.

"Oh, yes." Adam laughed softly, triumphantly. "You're so very ready for me, my passionate little darling."

Shay blushed fiercely, grateful for the darkness, which hid her inexperienced response to his frank observation.

"Shay, do you want me to take precautions?" His teeth nipped her lobe. "Or have you?"

Shay's heart thumped so loudly in her chest that she feared he might hear. Lying had never been her strong suit. "I'm—I'm all right, Adam."

"The Pill?"

"Mmmmm." She pulled his head down to hers.

"What in hell is going on here, Shay?"

Shay lay flat on her back and very, very still. A fine sheen of perspiration coated her body, and her hair lay across the pillow like a tangled silken web. It hadn't been so bad, she consoled herself. And the end result, if she was lucky, would be infinitely worth it. But first she had Adam to deal with, and at the moment he wasn't too pleased with her. To put it mildly.

Adam seized her chin in his hand and turned her head, forcing her to face him. She noted that his slate-gray eyes had again turned the color of gun-metal.

"What do you mean, Adam?"

"Don't play dumb with me, little girl. You were a virgin!"

It was an accusation, and a furious one at that. Shay swallowed and said nothing.

"Shay!" He obviously was not going to let the subject drop. "What do you have to say for yourself?"

"I hoped you wouldn't notice?" Shay offered hopefully.

"Don't try to be cute! I want some straight answers from you, lady. Now."

He really was angry, Shay thought with a sigh. And she wasn't sure how to deal with his anger. Not one of the books or magazines she'd read in preparation for this event had mentioned that a man might be livid to find he had just made love to a virgin.

"How did you know?" She stalled for time, being careful not to move. All the books had recommended lying flat for at least an hour afterward. "Was I that, er, inept?"

"Oh, you were fine in the beginning, a regular hot little number. It was only as we became—shall I say—more involved that your inexperience became evident. But I thought you were playing games and trying to back out, so I decided to teach you a lesson."

"Well, you did and I'm glad. It was a long-overdue one, at that."

"I'm not talking about taking your virginity, you little idiot!" He clenched his jaw. "Damn it, Shay, I must have hurt you. I was too fast and too rough for a virgin. I didn't know that you were having physical difficulty admitting me. If I'd known I could have—"

"If you'd known you would have been out the door like a shot," Shay said flatly. "That's why I didn't mention it. You weren't all that enthusiastic in the first place. It wasn't until much, much later that you decided you might want me."

Adam stared at her, dumbfounded.

"Did you think I hadn't noticed? I might have been a virgin but I'm not stupid. I practically had to drag you to bed."

Her frankness obviously floored him. "Then why did you persist?" He paused, frowning. "You must admit you *were* very persistent."

"Six weeks ago I celebrated my twenty-eighth birthday." Shay laid her fingers over his lips to stop him from making the comment always made when she revealed her age. "Don't tell me how young I look or how I could still pass for a teen-ager. I've heard it often enough, and it's entirely irrelevant. The fact is I was twenty-eight years old and still a virgin."

"So you decided to rectify the situation. But why me? Why drag me into your identity crisis?" He sat up and swung his legs over the side of the bed. Shay remained where she was, averting her gaze from his naked body. "I'm a veritable stranger to you, Shay. Isn't there someone else in your life, a boyfriend who—"

"I wanted you to be the one," she said softly. "Only you."

In the process of gathering his clothes, Adam paused to stare at her. "You mean you had this all planned?"

She nodded.

"For how long?"

It seemed safe enough to tell him the partial truth. His lawyer's instincts wouldn't be satisfied until he possessed what he considered to be a reasonable answer.

"I saw you for the first time about a month ago when I dropped off a needlepoint canvas at the Benningtons'. You were in the study with Bill, and I—I asked Catherine about you. I decided then that you were probably the one."

There was no need to mention the weeks spent

researching her theory. Her findings had backed up her initial response. Adam Prescott Wickwire III was the man to father her much-dreamed-of child.

"When I saw you again at Catherine and Bill's party, I knew it for certain. So I asked you here tonight."

Of course she hadn't been invited to the Benningtons' party; she was light years removed from their social circle. She'd learned of the party from Case, who had received an invitation. The Benningtons really did worship Case. They knew his surgical skills had saved their nine-year-old son's life following a serious automobile accident. Add to that Case's compassion and kindness toward the frightened, grieving relatives of all his patients, and a lifelong admiration had begun. The tri-state area included many people like the Benningtons, grateful relatives who considered Casey Flynn something of a god. A god to whom they sent dinner and party invitations, because of whom they donated money to the hospital's trauma unit and bought original needlepoint designs from his "baby sister" Shay.

Case had declined the invitation, of course. He had hardly any social life, choosing to devote almost his every waking hour to his patients in the trauma unit. But Shay had noted the date and decided it was time to realize her dream.

She had arrived at the Bennington house the evening of the party with another original needlepoint design that Catherine had ordered from her. Using every bit of acting ability she possessed, Shay had feigned surprise and embarrassment at arriving in the middle of a party. Catherine had reacted exactly as Shay had hoped. She'd insisted that Shay join the party. The introduction had been easily arranged when Shay expressed an interest in meeting the well-known Washington attorney Adam Wickwire. Catherine was only too happy to oblige.

"You asked me here for the express purpose of losing your virginity?" Adam raged, pulling on his clothes with unconcealed ire. "That's the most crazy, cold-blooded . . ." Words failed him, and he contented himself with glaring at her. That *he* should be the target of this weird little girl's single-minded plotting—and worse, that he should succumb to it—was both infuriating and appalling. Not to mention humiliating. Never had he been so blatantly used by a woman, he realized with a sudden flash of self-awareness, although he admitted with a twinge of guilt that he had used women himself. Still, he had always been honest in his dealings with the opposite sex, whereas this little cheat . . . A sudden thought struck him.

"Exactly what do you want from me, Shay?" His eyes glittered with shrewd savagery. "You're not about to let it end here, are you? What price am I going to have to pay for the"—he sneered—"gift of your virginity?"

"You think I'm going to ask you for money?" Shay gaped at him. "Are you kidding?"

She made him feel the complete fool. "I'm a rich man, lady. You must have wormed that much out of Catherine," he snarled. "I have an impeccable reputation in this city, and my family is an old and respected one. If you're intending to blackmail me, I can promise you that it won't wash."

"Blackmail you? Oh, never!" It hurt that he thought her capable of such treachery. "I admire you and your family too much to ever do anything to hurt you."

It was the truth. Shay found the Wickwires both admirable and impressive, so much so that she wanted her child to share their heritage. Adam Prescott Wickwire III, married for two years, divorced for ten, graduate of Andover, University of Virginia, Harvard Law School, honored for his academic and athletic skills; partner in the illustrious law firm of Wickwire, Prescott & Sinclair, which had been founded by his father and uncle.

Her research had borne out that Adam's intelligence more than matched his handsome face and imposing physique. And his family history was equally superior.

His father, Adam P. Wickwire, Jr., had left the law firm he'd founded with his brother-in-law and college roommate to become a district court judge, a position he still held. His mother was an accomplished equestrienne and committee chairwoman for a host of charities. The senior Wickwires lived on a rambling estate in Charlottesville, Virginia.

Adam's sister, purported to be as attractive and intelligent as Adam himself, was married and pursuing a career in advertising in New York City.

Perhaps most spectacular of all, Adam's three grandparents, in their mid-eighties, were alive and well and active. The one deceased grandfather would probably be around as well had he not taken a fatal fall from his horse—at the age of seventy-nine.

"So you chose me for the role of your first lover?" Adam towered over her, his face contorted with rage. He seemed to possess the primitive power of some ancient pagan god and Shay shivered involuntarily. Adam Wickwire was not a man to cross, not one to have as an enemy.

"Please don't be angry with me, Adam." Her dark blue eyes pleaded with him. He was completely dressed now, and she knew he was ready to walk out the door. But he couldn't leave now! The chances of a woman's becoming pregnant the first and only time she made love were slim; she didn't need a book to tell her that. And the awful things he had said to her, the cold way he looked at her . . .

"For God's sake, don't cry!" His voice was still harsh, but some of the anger had left his face.

"I'm not c-crying."

"No?" He sat down on the edge of the bed and touched her wet cheek. "And these aren't tears?"

Shay choked back a sob. She certainly hadn't intended to cry, but now it was difficult to hold back the tears. Somehow everything had slipped beyond her control. She'd never dreamed that Adam would be so angry and accusatory—or that his attitude would hurt her so.

"Shay, please don't cry." Adam's hands cupped her shoulders, his fingers stroking lightly. "Damn, I feel like a rat."

"No, no!" Shay protested, covering his hands with her own. Their fingers seemed to intertwine automatically. "You mustn't feel that way, Adam. I'll—I'll remember this night as long as I live." She sniffed delicately.

Adam heaved a sigh. "Make that a plague-carrying rat." His eyes met and held hers. "Shay, I'm sorry. I'm sorry for shouting at you and for making accusations I knew were untrue. We lawyers are a wary bunch, I'm afraid, and it was such a shock to learn you were a . . ."

"I know." Shay smiled up at him, her voice tremulous, relief singing in her veins. He wasn't angry with her anymore! "We aging virgins are an endangered species, probably blessedly close to extinction."

"A sexy little virgin." Adam's voice deepened. Slowly he lowered the sheet that she had pulled up to her chin during his tirade. "Seductive, passionate, who looked like a prim schoolmarm the first night I met her and a sultry sexpot tonight." His lips curved into a reminiscent smile. "Who doesn't even bother to wear underwear."

Shay blushed. "I really do, you know. This is the only time that I haven't."

"Somehow I guessed that." His thumb traced the curve of her mouth, parting her lips to glide along the smooth surface of her teeth. Shay drew in her breath sharply, and he took instant advantage, inserting his thumb in her mouth.

He exerted a firm, rhythmic pressure against her lower lip, and a piercing stab of sexual excitement shot through her.

"I've read that an innocent can be seduced by this very simple simulation," Adam murmured, his eyes sweeping the length of her body. "Is it true, Shay? Are you feeling this where you should?"

"Are you experimenting on me?" Shay tried to keep it light, but her voice shook. Yes, she was most definitely feeling the effects of Adam's touch.

He whispered a command and Shay mindlessly obeyed, closing her lips around his thumb to suck it. She stared dazedly into his eyes. Never had she felt so possessed, so totally dominated. Adam withdrew his thumb slowly, and for a long moment they gazed at each other.

"Adam." She watched in fascination as his mouth lowered to hers. Her lips parted at his touch, welcoming his tongue into the moist warmth within.

"My own passionate little virgin." Adam groaned huskily, releasing her mouth to blaze a trail of burning kisses along the slender curve of her neck. His hands moved over her urgently, insistently, as if he couldn't get enough of her.

"Stay with me, Adam." Shay sat up and tugged his coat from his shoulders. "Please don't leave me."

A sudden smile lit his face. "Just try to send me away."

She remembered at that moment that she should be lying flat and immediately lay back down. She had actually forgotten about her plans for a baby while she was begging Adam to stay!

Adam watched her, frowning his concern. "Shay, are you all right?"

She lay silently, every nerve ending tingling with an electric awareness. Adam lifted her hand to his cheek, and her palm smoothed over the chiseled hollow of his cheekbones, her fingertips examining the fine, strong features of his face.

"Shay, the first time is never the best." Adam caught her exploring hand and touched his mouth to her palm.

"Isn't it?" She saw the glimmer in his eyes, and her heart lurched. Again? Now? Wasn't it a bit too soon?

She tried to recall what the books had said, but her mind had gone blank.

"You look like a scared little girl, with those big blue eyes as round as saucers." He continued to hold her hand, stroking the sensitive palm with his thumb. "I'm not going to hurt you, Shay."

Shay gave herself a mental shake. She was failing miserably in her temptress role if he saw her as a scared little girl. She had to get her act together if she hoped to hold him for the rest of the weekend. "I'm not a scared little girl, Adam." Her voice quavered, and Shay bit her lower lip in vexation. Damn, she certainly sounded like one. She took a deep breath and tried again. "I'm a woman, with a woman's needs, who . . . who . . ." What was the rest of that line? It was a great one; Shay could even visualize the paperback it came from. "I'm a woman, with a woman's needs and desires," she began again determinedly.

Adam interrupted her, laughing. "Why do I have the feeling you're reciting some piece you've memorized?"

"I—I—wasn't!" Shay was aghast. Lawyers! They were far too cunning, far too perceptive. She rolled onto her stomach with a groan. "I've made a complete fool of myself, haven't I?"

"Sweetheart, no, of course not." Adam began to massage the taut muscles of her back. He was still chuckling, Shay noted grimly.

"Actually, I'm very impressed that you've gone to so much trouble to seduce me—your trip to the doctor for the pills, the fine wine, the dinner." Shay froze at his mention of the pills. "Relax, darling, I thoroughly approve. Can I assume that you also have some irresistibly sexy lingerie on hand to model for me?"

"Ohhh!" She buried her face in the pillow. She might as well confess; he would undoubtedly find it anyway. "There's a silk teddy hanging on the back of the bathroom door."

"Oh, Shay!" Adam laughed harder. "Come here, honey. Look at me."

Shay refused to budge. Things had gotten completely out of hand. How had her carefully orchestrated plans for seduction turned into a farce, with herself landing in the role of the hapless comic?

"Come here, baby." Adam turned her over and lifted her onto his lap. Shay was acutely, embarrassingly aware that he was fully dressed, while she was naked. Blushing, she reached for the sheet. Adam stopped her.

"I don't want you ever to feel shame with me, Shay," he said softly. He was no longer laughing; his eyes were a deep, dark gray. "And you needn't rely on some romantic script, complete with dialogue. Be real for me, Shay. Tell me what you want, what you like, what feels good. . . ."

He brushed his fingertips lightly over her nipples. "So hard and tight," he whispered, "and your breasts are so exquisitely soft."

Shay leaned heavily against him. Her eyelids fluttered shut as he gently brushed his lips over them, treating her forehead and her temple and her cheeks to the same feather-light caress. Her breasts were aching for his touch, but his fingers continued to torment her with fleeting little forays around her nipples. His lips heightened the torment by searing a path of tiny stinging kisses along her neck. A fiery urgency seemed to ignite every nerve, and, uttering a strangled cry, Shay seized his teasing hand and placed it firmly over one breast.

"Is this what you want, sweetheart?" Adam cupped the soft fullness, kneading and stroking until she whimpered with pleasure. "Does it feel good, Shay?"

"Oh, yes, Adam." She sighed. Her heart was throbbing like a jungle drum, and her head fell back in total abandon.

Adam's other large hand traveled along the curves of her waist and hips in long, slow strokes, then slipped possessively between her thighs. His mouth fastened over hers, and she responded with greedy passion.

He took off his clothes; she was too far gone to recall just how he managed. Shay was clinging as he eased her down onto the bed. He nudged her legs apart with his knee, and she shifted lanquidly to allow him to apply an exciting, erotic pressure.

"Don't be frightened, Shay." Adam spoke softly, soothingly. "This time will be good for you, darling. I promise."

"I'm not afraid, Adam," she breathed, smoothing her palms over the solid warmth of his back. It was true. She felt no fears, no inhibitions, only a glowing sense of rightness.

Time seemed to stand still as they kissed and caressed and nibbled and nipped, using fingers and lips, teeth and tongues, to feel and taste and pleasure each other. At last he moved on top of her, entering her slowly, soothing her with love words as he kissed her tenderly.

He was so understanding, so considerate and patient, Shay thought rapturously, acclimating her body slowly to the feel of his. "Oh Adam, it feels so wonderful. . . ." Her voice trailed off in embarrassed confusion. It was unlike her to blurt out her innermost thoughts like that.

"I know, love, it feels so good inside you." Adam kissed her again, fiercely. "We'll take it slow and easy, sweetheart."

He began to move within her, long, slow, deep strokes that made her gasp with pleasure.

"You like this very much, don't you?" Adam murmured against her ear, and Shay moaned an incoherent reply.

She was overpowered by the turbulent new sensations that seemed to build and build, that swept them both into a torrent of heady passion. Adam guided her through the swirling waters, and she clung to him as her body seemed to explode with a pleasure so intense that she cried out his name in astonished wonder. For long moments afterward she lay still, dazed by the ecstasy of what had happened.

When she finally opened her eyes she found Adam studying her intently.

"I loved seeing you flame like a torch in my arms." His smile held warmth and tenderness and pure masculine pride. "All those virginal restraints and inhibitions simply melted away. You are so very passionate, my darling."

None of her reading had prepared her for this. The thought swam groggily through her mind as she held Adam tightly. There were no words to describe the warm, secure feeling of oneness, the sense of completeness, the drowsy contentment of shared satiation.

Shay forgot about her carefully kept temperature charts, forgot about lying still for an hour, forgot about everything but holding Adam close in the sweet afterglow of passion. They kissed and caressed and talked softly until she fell asleep in his arms, still clinging tightly to him.

Two

It was a shock to wake up with a man in her bed.
Even more shocking was the position of total abandon in which she found herself: sprawled over Adam,
her arms and legs entwined with his, her long hair
streaming over his chest like a silken cover. Shay
raised her head and met Adam's slate-gray eyes. Neither spoke for several long minutes.

"I thought last night might have been a dream,"
Adam said at last. "But here is my dream girl, in my
arms."

Shay watched him, searching for some sort of clue
as to how to play this scene. Flippant or sincere?
Seductive or—

"No acting, Shay." Adam cupped her chin in his
hand and gazed into the depths of her eyes. "Be honest with me."

"What do you mean?" His perception alarmed her.
It was as if he had looked into her mind and seen her
dilemma.

"No, I'm not a mind-reader. Your face is just very
expressive." He smiled, startling her further. "I see a
sensitive young woman who is feeling particularly

vulnerable and is unsure of what to do or say next. There's no need, darling. Be Shay, my lover of last night."

Shay forced a tight little smile. "You make me feel transparent, Adam. I must be boringly predictable to you."

"Boring!" Adam laughed. "I don't think you could be boring if you tried, Shay. To be perfectly frank, I find you fascinating. I've never met a woman like you before in my life."

Shay wasn't sure if he was being complimentary. Fascinating covered a lot of ground, not all of it positive.

"Is breakfast on the agenda?" Adam untangled himself from her and sat up in bed. "I'm starving, woman."

"Worked up a healthy appetite during the night, hmm?" Shay grinned at him. "Yes, the plans included breakfast in bed if—" She broke off abruptly. She musn't tell him too much. It was becoming increasingly easy to confide in him, and if she were to accidentally let slip her motives for luring him here . . .

"If?" Adam prompted gently. "Don't clam up on me, Shay."

"If you stayed the night," she heard herself tell him. "I hoped you would, but I couldn't be sure. I might have, you know, turned you off or . . ."

Shut up, Shay! she admonished herself severely. The bedroom was not the place to unload her insecurities. She should be breezy, cool. She pasted a determined smile on her face. "That is, I—"

"Turned me off? Not a chance, Shay." Adam drew her into his arms for a deep, lingering kiss, a kiss filled more with tenderness than passion.

A dangerous kiss, Shay knew, for it went beyond mere sex into the realm of involvement and caring. And that was not in her plans. She didn't want an affair with Adam Wickwire; she wanted his child. Yet she couldn't seem to drag herself out of his arms. She cuddled against him, basking in the tender warmth of his kiss.

"I'd better fix your breakfast." Shay gave him a shaky smile when he finally released her. "How do you like your eggs?"

"Fried. Over easy."

"Bacon or sausage?"

"Bacon. Very crisp but not burned."

"I never burn the bacon," she informed him saucily, tossing her head. Her sable-colored hair cascaded down her back.

Adam watched her walk across the room, his eyes gleaming. "Shay, are you going to put on your sexy little teddy for me?"

"Of course. It comes with the breakfast."

Wearing the deep purple teddy—the high cut at the thigh emphasizing her long, shapely legs and the low-cut lacy bodice accentuating the full firmness of her breasts—Shay served Adam breakfast in bed. Freshly squeezed orange juice, two fried eggs over easy, crisp bacon, toasted English muffin with butter and home-made strawberry jam, and coffee. Leaving him with the tray, she returned to the kitchen and brought back a plate for herself.

"Delicious." Adam sighed appreciatively. "You didn't even break the yolks."

"Of course not."

"You're an excellent cook, Shay. Is that because of the old adage, 'The way to a man's heart is through his stomach'?"

"Because of necessity. My mother's idea of a home-cooked meal was to open a can of tuna and hand you a fork. I learned to cook as soon as I learned to read, and took over the kitchen."

"Very resourceful," Adam said approvingly. "Tell me more about yourself, Shay."

She was instantly on guard. "More?"

"It's strange," he said musingly. "I feel I know you

very well, yet I actually know few facts about your life. I want to know more, Shay."

"What do you want to know? My zodiac sign? My hobbies? My favorite television show? We're not in a singles' bar, Adam. I hate this kind of superficial patter."

"Normally, so do I but—"

"Suppose I told you that I'm a Scorpio, that my hobbies are surfing and hang-gliding and my favorite thing to watch on television is *Ozzie and Harriet* reruns. Would that satisfy your curiosity?"

"Lies, all lies." Adam grinned. "You've already told me that your birthday was six weeks ago so that makes you a Leo. No one in Washington surfs, and you don't strike me as the hang-gliding type."

She raised an eyebrow. "What about *Ozzie and Harriet*? Are you afraid that part might be true?"

Adam laughed. She loved to hear him laugh, Shay admitted to herself, gazing at him. He had been so serious, so reserved those first times she had seen him, including the early part of the night before. Until she had gotten him into bed. He hadn't been at all reserved then; he had given fully of himself.

"What's that Mona Lisa smile for?"

Refocusing on Adam, Shay noticed that he was staring at her, studying her closely. He always seemed to be watching her, she thought. He seldom took his eyes off her.

He had finished his breakfast, and Shay rose to take the tray. "I was just remembering how formal you were at the beginning of last night . . . and how you weren't later."

She expected him to make some flippant comeback that she would counter with one of her own. Instead he grew serious, his gray eyes thoughtful.

"Last night was a revelation to me, Shay. The feelings you evoked in me . . . I'm not sure how to put it without sounding corny or adolescent, but last night I discovered a passion that I never knew I had, never knew I was capable of. Does that make any sense to you?"

Shay turned away from him to set the tray on top of the bureau. She mustn't let him continue; after today she would never see him again. She wanted his baby and he seemed to be saying he wanted an affair with her. The two were mutually incompatible goals. It was time to inject a light note before things became too complicated.

"Now who's spouting dialogue from a romantic novel?" she teased. It took great effort to produce the necessary winsome grin. What she really wanted to do, she realized with a start, was to lock herself in the bathroom and cry.

Adam frowned. "Do you really believe I'm handing you a line, Shay?"

"I don't know," she whispered. "It would be easier if you were."

"Come to me, Shay." Adam extended his hand to her. Shay took it and allowed him to draw her down on the bed, into his arms. "Maybe I'm going too fast for you." He fitted her into the hard curve of his body, stroking her long hair with gentle hands. "Don't worry, darling. I'll give you all the time you need."

Shay snuggled closer. "Will you stay with me today, Adam?"

"I can stay till one, honey." He glanced at his watch. "That gives us almost three hours together." His big hands moved slowly over the silken purple teddy. "You look so damn sexy in this thing, but how do I get it off?"

Shay moved sinuously against him. "I think I'll let you figure that out for yourself, Mr. Phi Beta Kappa."

Adam groaned huskily, and his mouth closed over hers. The tides of their passion swirled and crested, carrying them both to the heights of ecstasy and finally breaking in a wild, shimmering shared release.

Afterward, they talked for a while, a drowsy, languid conversation punctuated by long kisses. They slept and awoke and made love again. At some point in the afternoon, Shay staggered to the kitchen to heat some canned soup, which they ate in the bedroom. And then they made love for the third (or was it the fourth? Shay lost count somewhere along the line) time that day.

"Adam, it's six o'clock," Shay murmured softly. She was lying in his arms, her head on his shoulder, their limbs comfortably, intimately entwined.

"It can't be," Adam groaned. "I've never spent an entire day in bed before. Excluding illness, of course."

"You said you had to leave at one," Shay reminded him. "It's long past that now."

"Funny how you can lose all track of time when you're involved with . . . other things." Adam smiled lazily. "What's even funnier is that it's never happened to me before. I've lived by the clock since my kindergarten days."

He shifted slightly, and Shay forced herself to sit up. It was time, she knew, and a cold vise seemed to grip her heart. Given the proper biological conditions and the numerous opportunities, it was likely that her child had been conceived.

It was time to send Adam Wickwire on his way. Her reluctance to do so alarmed her.

"I was supposed to make an appearance at the Maclaines' pool party this afternoon," Adam continued, stroking her bare arm lightly. "But I'm so glad I stayed here with you." His hand settled possessively on her hip, his fingers splaying over her stomach's smooth flatness.

"Maclaine?" Shay inched slowly away from him. "The senator?"

"Yes." Adam caught her and hauled her back against him. "Our families are old friends."

"I'm impressed." Shay began to struggle. "Adam, I want to get up."

"Kiss me first."

"No, Adam, I—"

He flipped her onto her back, pinning her firmly against the mattress with the warm weight of his body. "No?" He was smiling in a way that made her weak, and his eyes were warm and caressing. "That's the first time I've heard that word from you, my insatiable little lover. Now, kiss me or I'll keep you here all night."

Her arms circled his neck, and she raised her mouth to his. It was the last time she would ever kiss him. The knowledge pierced her heart, making her want to cry out in pain. She didn't want to let him go!

"Why don't we go out for dinner?" Adam released her and climbed out of bed.

"No, Adam." Shay pulled the sheet over her, clutching it with icy fingers. Her throat was dry and tight, and her heart seemed to be thundering in her ears.

"Sweetie, you've fixed me three meals already. It's my turn to feed you."

Shay watched him gather his clothes, so blithely unaware of what was to come. She fought back the sudden urge to burst into tears. "Adam, I want you to leave."

He stopped and stood stock-still, watching her. For a moment Shay nearly lost her nerve, almost succumbed to the irresistible urge to reach out her arms to him. But she did not.

"Please go, Adam. I—I'm tired." It sounded weak and whiney to her own ears, but she couldn't seem to summon the force necessary to purposefully eject him.

"What's this all about, Shay?" Adam's voice was dangerously quiet.

"I just want to be alone. I—I need to be alone!"

"Darling, what is it?" He dropped his clothes and strode across the room. "You can tell me." He sat down on the edge of the bed, but Shay rolled on her side away from him.

"I don't want to talk, Adam. I just want you to leave."

"The hell I will!" He pulled her round to face him. "I want to know what's going on in that unfathomable little mind of yours, Shay."

"Let me go!" Shay's voice rose shrilly, and she felt hot tears well in her eyes. This weekend had given her a glimpse of something she had never known, had never dreamed of, but it was something she could never have. "Why can't you just go away and leave me alone!"

"This is unbelievable!" Adam stood up and snatched his clothes, then stormed furiously into the small bathroom.

Shay heard him turn on the taps in the shower and hopped out of bed, racing to the closet, where she retrieved a canvas overnight bag. She removed her clothes from it, quickly pulling on a lilac bra and panties, blue jeans, a purple-and-white striped shirt, and a pair of well-worn black ballet slippers. She brushed her hair, wincing as she tugged at the tangles, finally securing it on both sides with a pair of bright purple enamel barrettes. She paused in front of the mirror and glanced at her reflection. She looked like herself again; the alluring seductress was gone.

Adam emerged from the bathroom, fully dressed, his dark hair still slightly damp from the shower. In his expensive, conservative clothing he looked the epitome of the successful, sophisticated, blue-blooded Washington attorney. Which, of course, he was.

How different they were! His gaze traveled over her, and Shay guessed he was seeing her as she really was—the slightly offbeat nonconformist from the wrong side of town. Which, of course, she was. A woman he would never willingly choose as the mother of his child. He must never, ever know. . . .

"I won't pretend that I'm not baffled by your sudden about-face," Adam began stiffly, then walked across the room and grasped her upper arms. "Shay, for God's sake, talk to me. I can't leave you like this! This weekend—"

"—is over," she finished flatly, pulling away from him.

Her response infuriated an already volatile Adam. "Do you know what I want to do? What I ought to do? Strip you and toss you down on that bed and make love to you until you're incapable of thought! It shouldn't take too long to reach that point, should it, Shay? I've already had you mindless and begging quite a few times this weekend, haven't I?"

Shay colored painfully. "Please don't, Adam."

"Now, that is a different tune. Earlier it was 'Please, Adam,' 'Make love to me, Adam.' Where's the hot little tease who couldn't wait to jump into bed? You can't turn back now, Shay." He wanted to hurt her, he realized, astonished by the force of his anger. He wanted to make her cry, to reduce her to a state of pleading, sobbing helplessness. And then he would take her in his arms and . . .

"I know you must hate me, Adam," Shay said softly.

"Hate you? Damn it, Shay, I don't hate you! How could I ever hate you?" He heaved an exasperated sigh. "Are you putting yourself through some weird guilt trip? You couldn't possibly believe that antiquated notion that a man can't respect the woman he's taken to bed?"

Shay twisted her hands uncertainly. Suppose she let him assume that?

Adam was incredulous. "My God, you do!"

"We Irish might not have invented guilt"—she forced a small smile—"but we've elevated it to an art form."

"Oh, honey." Adam took her in his arms and held her close. "I think I understand. You were trying to drive me away first because you fully expected never to hear from me again."

Shay could almost hear his thoughts fall into place. Lawyers liked things orderly and reasonable and attempted to fit everything into a logical, analytical pattern. Now that he thought he understood the reason for her sudden behavior change, he was prepared to deal with it.

"You have nothing to worry about, Shay." He drew a pen and one of his business cards from a pocket inside his suit coat. "I'm going to write down your phone number and call you tomorrow." He proceeded to copy the number printed on the telephone. "In fact, I'll call you tonight. Around eleven?"

Shay watched him write down the number, knowing that when he dialed it he would reach Dr. Casey Flynn's answering machine. Her own telephone number was unlisted.

"Let's go out to eat." Adam was smiling now. "Are there any good restaurants around here?"

"There are a couple of fast food places down the street," Shay said, shrugging. Actually, she was unfamiliar with this part of the city. She seldom visited her brother here at his apartment. They usually met at the hospital or at her place.

"Oh, well, why not?" Adam clasped a hand around the nape of her neck and propelled her to the door. "I promise to take you to a four-star restaurant tomorrow, honey."

They ate at a Burger King and walked across the street to a crowded Dairy Queen stand for a frozen custard afterward. Adam was obviously relaxed and happy, and Shay couldn't take her eyes off him. This was the end, she warned herself as they walked hand in hand back to the apartment, licking the fast-melting ice cream as they went. He didn't have her phone number, and he didn't know where she lived or worked. She had mentioned that she enjoyed painting, but she hadn't added that she was the art teacher at Carver High School.

He wouldn't be able to find her. Of course he could ask the Benningtons or her brother, but she knew he wouldn't. The Wickwire pride would prevent him from revealing to anyone that he had been duped.

Adam walked her to the door of Case's apartment,

stepping inside with her for one last passionately tender kiss.

"Good night, Shay," he murmured, his eyes glowing with a promise she knew would never be fulfilled.

"Good night, Adam."

From the window she watched him get into his gray Mercedes and drive away with a jaunty little farewell blast on the horn. The urge to weep was almost overwhelming, but Shay resolutely resisted it. She would have her baby, she consoled herself as she cleaned up the kitchen and washed and dried all the dishes.

She must think positively. Both the calendar and Adam's obvious virility rendered a child a strong possibility. Yes, there would be a baby, there had to be!

Shay stuffed the purple teddy, velvet skirt, and plum silk blouse into the canvas bag. Her own baby—it would be a dream come true. How she would love her child, boy or girl. It would never know the pain of rejection or the unhappiness of living with two parents who hated each other. Shay and her brother and sister had; she was determined to do it better.

She gathered up the pretty sheets, the quilt, and the pillows and pushed them into a large plastic bag. She and her baby would be a *real* family, a tightly knit unit of love and security. Locking the door to her brother's apartment, Shay carried her case and the bulging plastic bag to the old blue Buick parked at the curb.

Tonight she would tell her brother that she had used his apartment while he was on call at the hospital. Of course she wouldn't mention why or with whom, nor would he ask. The torrid, passionate, and totally wonderful weekend with Adam was her own secret, just as the child she knew she carried was hers alone.

Three

"This just isn't doing what I want it to do, Miss Flynn." The pretty black teenager frowned at the painting on the easel before her.

Shay crossed the school art room to stand behind the girl and study her painting. "I don't see any problem whatsoever, Tiana. What do you think is wrong with it?"

"Oh, I don't know." Tiana laid down her brush with a sigh. "Too much green, maybe? I guess I just haven't got it today."

"We all feel like that sometimes, Tiana," Shay said soothingly. "Why not leave it for a while and come back to it later? You might have a whole new perspective by then."

"You wouldn't have something else for me to do while I'm waiting for this new perspective, would you, Miss Flynn?" The girl's dark eyes danced impishly. "Something like painting barrettes for the Arts and Crafts Show?"

"Tiana, you're always one step ahead of me." Shay grinned. "We'll need plenty for the show."

"I'll start painting." Tiana pretended to grumble as

she reached for a bag of metal barrettes. Painted in bright enamel colors, sometimes with initials and designs as well, the barrettes were popular at school, and Shay was certain they would sell quite well at the Art Show.

Another girl came running up to Shay. "Something's burning, Miss Flynn. I think it's the salt dough."

Shay rushed into the tiny back room, which accommodated an old electric stove and an equally ancient refrigerator.

"I got it, Miss Flynn." A boy of about fourteen removed a tray of salt-dough bears from the oven.

"Thanks, Jerad," she said, breathing a sigh of relief. She inspected the bears. "They're a little crisper than usual, but we can still use them." She turned to the small group of students who crowded around her. "Who wants to paint them?"

"I'll do it, Miss Flynn." A tall thin girl with huge, dark eyes raised her hand.

Shay smiled warmly at the girl. Chandra Washington was always the first to volunteer for any project. "Thank you, Chandra. They'll make super Christmas tree ornaments when they're done."

As the students returned to their work in the larger room, Shay looked around with satisfaction. She had formed the Art Club six years ago, not long after assuming the position of art teacher at this enormous inner-city junior-senior high school. Teaching such large groups made it difficult to establish even a minimal relationship with each student, so she had taken it upon herself to form the club as an extracurricular activity. She volunteered her Tuesdays and Wednesdays after school as the club's adviser and was pleased with the students' response, which increased each year. There was an astonishing amount of talent in some of these youngsters, which burst into bloom under her interested and caring tutelage.

"Mr. Deroy is here, Miss Flynn," Tiana sang out as

a tall, moustached man in blue jeans and a plaid work shirt entered the room. He carried a large brown paper bag.

"I've got sodas for all you thirsty artists," he announced, and was promptly swamped by enthusiastic students.

Shay watched with a smile. Paul Deroy, the school's guidance counselor, was always a welcome visitor in any department. In his early thirties, he had come to Carver High two years ago and was well liked by both students and teachers.

"Would you like one, Shay?" Paul offered her a can as he joined her near the kiln in the corner.

"No thanks, Paul. I've given up caffeine." Automatically Shay's hand went to her abdomen, where her baby rested, as yet undetectable. She had read in one of the weekly newsmagazines that caffeine was considered to be a risk for the unborn and had immediately eliminated it from her diet.

"You're stronger than I am." Paul grinned. "I'd kill for my morning coffee."

"It was nice of you to bring sodas for the kids," Shay said as she watched the students drain the contents of the cans. "They've been working so hard, with the show only a month away and Christmas three weeks after that!"

"Your Arts and Crafts Show is the talk of the school." Paul gazed admiringly at her. "Of the whole school district, really. You've worked wonders with these kids, Shay. The atmosphere in this room is the envy of every principal in the area."

Shay shrugged, uncomfortable as always with lavish praise.

"Art's fun, Paul. I doubt if I'd be such a hit with the kids if I taught something like government or trig."

Paul laughed. "You're far too modest. But the administration here knows what it has, and we're fiercely possessive of you. There's no way we'll allow you to be lured to the magnet school in Anacostia or, worse, to one of the suburban schools."

"I have no intention of leaving, Paul," she assured him.

His smile faded. "Not even if you and your husband, ah, get back together?" He made a wry grimace. "Forgive me, Shay. Feel free to tell me to mind my own business."

"Nothing definite has been decided, Paul," Shay said quietly. She didn't like to lie, but she'd invented the fiction of an estranged husband when she'd first begun to dream of single motherhood, nearly five years ago. It served as an escape hatch as well. If a man she was dating began to sound too serious, as Paul Deroy once had, she brought out the husband and the prospect of a reconciliation.

Paul continued to stare at her wistfully. Shay knew he liked her very much. And she liked him—too much to risk hurting him by becoming involved with him. If she'd chosen him to be the father of her child, all sorts of complications would have ensued, not the least being his inevitable insistence on marrying her. Shay shuddered at the thought. Marriage was something she meant to live without. Her parents' miserable union had convinced her, and Case and Candy as well, that marriages were made—and existed—in hell.

At about six that evening Shay was busy working in her apartment when her doorbell rang. She grimaced. She was putting the finishing touches on a bright tulip-pattern needlepoint canvas, and whoever was at the door would just have to wait a bit. This design was one of her most popular, and Sally Vasey, owner of a small Georgetown needlework boutique, had ordered six, along with six other assorted hand-painted canvases. The canvases sold remarkably well, at prices that never ceased to astonish Shay. What had begun as a hobby to exercise her talents and earn a little extra money had blossomed into a lucrative second career. Even if she took a year of unpaid maternity leave, Shay was confident she could support herself and her child.

"Just a minute!" she shouted when the doorbell rang again, concentrating on completing one last tulip.

Outside her door, Adam Wickwire clenched his fists in anger. He was angry with Shay for making him wait one moment longer to see her and angry with himself at the tingle that shot through him at the sound of her voice. It had been two months, two weeks, and three days since he'd last heard that voice, and he'd spent that time alternating between wanting to tear the city apart to find her and trying desperately to forget that their incredible weekend together had ever happened.

When he hadn't been successful in the latter attempt, he'd convinced himself that he had to see her one more time. He would either persuade her that she had nothing to fear from their relationship or prove to himself that she wasn't as special, as spectacular, as wonderfully warm and sexy as he remembered her.

Growling with frustration, he pushed the doorbell again.

"All right, all right," Shay called through the door. He heard the lock click, then the door swung open.

"Hello, Shay."

The breath seemed to be sucked out of her lungs as Shay stared up into Adam Wickwire's gunmetal gray eyes. For a moment she stood stock-still, too shocked to move or even utter a syllable.

He appeared taller then she had remembered, his shoulders broader, and the perfectly tailored tan suit accentuated every aspect of his powerful frame. But she must have memorized every feature of his face, for the clear gray eyes, with their thick, dark lashes, the sensual mouth, and strong chin were vividly familiar to her.

"How did you find me?" she managed to choke out.

"It wasn't easy," Adam returned coolly. "You covered your tracks well, Shay. An unlisted phone, an unknown address. You were determined never to see me again, weren't you?"

"You're so perceptive!"

"Why, Shay?"

The bile rose in her throat. "Adam, don't ask me questions I can't answer."

"Suppose I answer for you?" He stepped inside, forcing her to back into her small living room. "I thought I had helped you not to feel guilty over our weekend together, but obviously I hadn't. You were determined to punish yourself . . . and me."

"You're wrong." Shay twisted her hands in a nervous gesture that belied her words. "I—I don't—didn't feel the least bit guilty."

"No?" Adam closed the door and leaned against it casually. "Have dinner with me and we'll talk about it, Shay."

"It would be a waste of time," Shay replied tersely. "I don't think so."

"No, Adam." She strolled nonchalantly across the room, pretending to be absorbed in one of her paitings hanging on the wall.

"I won't take 'no' for an answer, Shay. Not after all the trouble I went through to find you."

She turned back to him. "How *did* you find me?" she asked, her curiosity momentarily defeating her resolve to remain cold and indifferent.

"Through the Benningtons. Catherine was positively delighted to ask your brother for your address. I never realized what an avid matchmaker she is."

"You asked . . . Catherine? I—I never dreamed that you would."

"I had to see you again, Shay. That need finally overcame my pride." The quiet determination in his voice unnerved her. "I want you to have dinner with me tonight."

Shay considered it, frowning. The set of Adam's jaw brooked no argument. Perhaps it would be best to give in to him now. She looked the same now, but her pregnancy would soon begin to show. Better that they have dinner this night, and she would make certain it was the last meal they'd ever share. This was going to be the worst date Adam Prescott Wickwire III had ever had!

"All right, I'll have dinner with you tonight." Shay put just the right touch of sulky resignation in her voice. "But I'll have to change." She indicated her faded jeans and paint-splattered work shirt.

"Take your time." Adam smiled, generous in victory. The indulgence in his tone set Shay's teeth on edge.

She marched into her bedroom and closed the door, then surveyed the contents of her wardrobe with a thoughtful frown. Which outfit would offend Adam's conservative tastes the most? After a few moments of careful deliberation, she teamed a bright purple turtleneck and matching tights with an electric orange miniskirt.

The effect was startling, and Shay winced as she caught sight of herself in the mirror. The orange mini was an ancient hand-me-down from her sister, a relic of Candy's wild days in the sixties. Of course her sister probably had never worn it with purple, not even then.

Slipping into the high-heeled sandals she had worn for the first and only time that evening with Adam, Shay reached for her makeup bag. She made a spectacular job of it. Thick purple eyeshadow and gobs of mascara. Equally heavy-handed applications of rouge and dark plum lipstick. Her hairstyle took some thought, but she came up with a winner. Fastening the thick sable tresses atop her head with an elastic band, she braided five different colors of yarn through her hair, creating a magnificent rainbow plait. For a finishing touch, she affixed large gold hoop earrings to her ears.

Shay viewed the overall effect with malicious glee. She looked like a hooker, and a cheap one at that. A man of Adam Wickwire's tastes and position would rather die than be seen in public with the likes of her. He would take one look at her and run!

"Shay?" Adam's expression was one of classic shock as he gazed at the creature who came through the bedroom door.

Shay stifled the urge to giggle at his stupefaction. To her great disappointment, Adam recovered almost immediately.

"I thought we were going to dinner"—his eyes flicked over her from head to foot—"not to trick-or-treat."

"You don't like my outfit?" Shay blinked innocently.

"I liked your seductress costume much better. What do you call this one?"

Damn, she hadn't expected him to react with humor. She'd been so certain that he would be disgusted and stomp away in anger. To her further annoyance, Adam walked past her, through the tiny kitchen, and into her bedroom/studio.

"Do you mind?" she asked waspishly, following him a little unsteadily in her high heels. "This isn't a house tour, you know."

His gaze swept over the easels and brushes and paints, the wooden work table and stool, finally coming to rest on the double bed in the corner. "Haven't I seen that quilt before?"

Shay willed herself not to blush and failed utterly. She averted her eyes and refused to answer him.

"It was in your brother's apartment that night. Those pillow shams, too. Who could forget all that purple? Shay, did you bring them to the bedroom—"

"Yes," she snapped, deciding to seize the offensive. "I did. Casey's room looks like a monk's cell, and in the "Guide to a Sensuous Bedroom" it said to . . ." Her voice trailed off. She hadn't meant to reveal her sources.

"The sensuous bedroom," Adam repeated. He was silent for a few long moments, his gaze shifting from the bed to Shay, who stood in the doorway as if poised for flight. When he spoke again, his tone was dry. "I take it seduction will not be on the agenda tonight?"

"It certainly won't!"

"I didn't think so." He began to walk toward her, and she jumped away, scurrying into the living room like a frightened rabbit. "Relax, Shay. I'm not about to *ravish* you!"

She hated the sardonic smile, which made her blush yet again.

"The last time was very much at your insistence, if you'll recall."

"That's over and done with," Shay managed to say in a tight little voice. He was so tall, and the trim cut of his suit emphasized the breadth of his shoulders and his muscular thighs. An image of him standing nude before her flashed unexpectedly in her mind's eye. She could remember the texture of his hair-roughened skin, the musky, masculine scent that was his alone. Her knees weakened and she grasped the back of the couch, suddenly breathless.

They had made a baby that weekend. The thought spun giddily through her brain. He had used his strength and his virility to pleasure her . . . and to give her a child.

"Don't be afraid of me, Shay." Adam's voice was husky and deep as he walked over to her and stood uncomfortably close.

Shay felt the heat emanating from his body, smelled the familiar scent of him, and went limp with wanting. Only a few inches and she would be in his arms . . .

Her horrifying urge to take that step broke the spell of sensuality threatening to overwhelm her.

"I'm not afraid of you!" she folded her arms across her chest. "But I don't want to have dinner with you."

Adam seemed maddeningly deaf to her refusal. "I have reservations at the Lion d'Or." He paused significantly. "But I don't think we'll be able to keep them."

"Why not?" Shay knew the Lion d'Or. Candy and Case had taken her to dinner there. The patrons and the waiters in that posh establishment would be pop-eyed at the sight of her in her outlandish outfit. "That's just where I want to go."

"If you'll wash off the war paint and change into something more, uh, suitable, I'll take you there, Shay."

"I'm not changing, Adam. If you want to take me out to dinner, you'll have to take me as I am." She lowered her head to conceal the smile that played across her face. "After all, I dressed very carefully for this date."

"How true." He chuckled. "Did you study a collection of pictures of punk rockers for inspiration?"

Shay fought the inclination to laugh in return. Sharing his joke suddenly seemed the most natural thing in the world. She shook her head. She was trying to get rid of the man, not encourage him! She must make herself as alienating as the clothes she wore. "Are we going to the Lion d'Or or not?"

"Honey, be reasonable. If we walk into the place with you decked out like a dollar-an-hour street-walker, we'll—"

"Are you ashamed to be seen with me, Adam?"

Adam sighed. "Shay, I'm beginning to lose patience with you. You've had your little joke, and now it's time to—"

"It's no joke, Adam," she interrupted again. "If you're ashamed to be seen with me, then I won't go out with you."

She saw the irritation lurking in his eyes and watched in fascination as he carefully schooled his features into a smooth mask of equanimity.

"I saw an interesting little Italian restaurant just a few blocks from here." His tone was as bland as his expression. "Why don't we go there?"

"To Tony's?"

"Yes, I believe that was the name of the place."

"Are you crazy?" Shay asked in a shrill voice, beginning to enjoy this game immensely. "Somebody from the neighborhood might be there. I don't want anybody I know to see me dressed like a hooker."

Adam drew a deep breath. "Shay, are you deliberately trying to infuriate me?"

"Of course. Am I succeeding?"

"Extremely well." A muscle twitched convulsively in his jaw.

"Then why don't you leave? You don't have to take this kind of abuse from a nobody like me."

"No, I don't!" He strode toward the door, and Shay gave a sigh of relief. The relief was short-lived, for Adam turned suddenly and began to laugh.

"Very good, Shay. I admire your tactics. You almost managed to make me angry enough to go slamming out of here."

"Well, why don't you?" She leaned back against the couch, frustrated.

"Because I want to have dinner with you." Adam heaved a weary sigh. "Shay, is that really too much to ask of you? A simple dinner together?"

He seemed so genuinely disappointed by her steadfast refusal to spend the evening with him, that Shay almost felt sorry for him. Almost, but not quite.

"You know my terms, Adam."

"That we go to the Lion d'Or with you dressed as you are," Adam stated, and Shay nodded in agreement. "And you won't go to Tony's dressed as you are," he added, and Shay shook her head. "It seems that we've arrived at an impasse with only one solution."

"We break the date," Shay suggested eagerly.

"Wrong. We stay here." Adam dropped into an overstuffed lavender armchair. "Are you going to cook or shall we order out?"

"You can't stay here!" Shay gasped at the sheer audacity of the man. "And I'm certainly not going to cook for you!"

"All right, we'll send out for food. Italian, Mexican, or Chinese?" He grinned up at her, reminding her of a sly jungle cat daring its prey to move closer.

"You can't stay here!" she repeated furiously.

"Can't I?"

"No! Now, leave! Immediately!"

"And if I don't? What then, Shay? Will you throw me out bodily? Maybe call the police and have them do it?" He gave a feral smile. "Somehow I don't think so."

"You're impossible!"

"And so are you. An ideal match, it seems."

Shay flounced out of the living room, trembling with the force of her anger and aware that Adam had stood up and was following her. He was right, of course. There was no way she could physically remove him from her apartment. She had tried her best to drive him away, but for some inexplicable and unfathomable reason, he had chosen not to go.

She stalked through the kitchen, but, unaccustomed to the height of her heels, was thrown off balance when she collided with the kitchen table. She started to fall and tried to stop herself, but Adam caught her, grasping her shoulders and pulling her upright. For a moment Shay leaned back against him, her heart pounding as she instinctively clutched her abdomen.

She could have fallen and hurt the baby! She was a fool to behave so recklessly, to take such chances with her precious child's safety. Angrily she kicked off the shoes and was suddenly four and a half inches shorter, a smaller and more vulnerable five six to Adam's imposing six two.

"You've shrunk before my very eyes." Adam's arms tightened around her, and he chuckled huskily, his lips somewhere in the vicinity of her temple. She felt his hard, warm strength as he pulled her closer, felt his hands smooth over her body, molding her tightly against his length. She inhaled deeply and felt drugged by the heady scent of him.

"No," she whispered, but Adam seemed not to have heard. He continued to hold her, to caress her with his big hands.

"You nearly fell, Shay," he murmured, his lips now brushing the soft curve of her neck. "Are you all right, honey?"

"Yes," she breathed. But she wasn't all right. The shuddering weakness coursing through her, the delicious warmth between her legs, the nipples taut and swollen and aching to be touched—it was all wrong.

He nibbled sensuously on her lobe, his lips colliding briefly with the huge gold hoop. He deftly removed it, then sank his teeth into the soft flesh.

"Adam, don't," she whispered shakily as a hundred, then a thousand, erotic shock waves pulsed through her.

Adam paid no heed. "I want you, Shay," he said in an unsteady voice as his hand moved upward to cup her breast, a breast made fuller and more sensitive by her pregnancy. "I've wanted you so badly and I couldn't find you. Even now I can hardly believe I have you in my arms." He gently massaged her breast with his palm, and she quivered.

"You like this, don't you?" He ran his thumb over the hardening tip of her breast. "I remembered how you moaned when I first touched you there."

Shay moaned again, and Adam laughed huskily in triumph. Seconds later his hands slid under her jersey to caress the smooth, bare skin of her midriff. The thin, stretchy material of her bra clung to her like a second skin, offering no protection against the sensual probing of his fingertips. A fire seemed to burn through her veins, and she pressed herself back against him.

"You're very sensitive there," Adam whispered as two of his long fingers dipped inside her bra to find the nipple taut and aching for him. "And so very responsive."

A wild, primitive excitement rocked her body and sent her reeling. The sexual awakening that had begun slowly and hesitantly that first time with Adam, which had then burst into mature, feminine arousal during that magic weekend, was heightened by the bodily changes and demands of pregnancy. She needed him, she admitted to herself. She needed him so much.

Shay sighed as he released the front clasp of her bra and took the soft, full weight of her breasts in his palms. His thumb and forefinger captured one nipple and played it with a slow, sensual rhythm.

"Oh, Adam," Shay gasped. She suddenly whirled around, tangling her fingers in the springy thickness of his dark hair and urging his mouth down to hers. His tongue invaded her mouth hungrily, and Shay reveled in the thrilling sensations she had thought she'd never feel again.

She didn't bother to protest when he swept her up in his arms, carrying her to the bedroom and laying her gently down on the patterned quilt. All rational thought had fled, leaving the voluptuous emotions surging through her in full command of her mind and body.

"You've haunted me for the past two months, Shay," Adam murmured as he feathered kisses along her throat. "I've relived that weekend with you so many times."

"Have you, Adam?" Shay said breathlessly. Oh, so had she, so many times. The stunning force of those memories had shown her how very easy it would be to become attached to this man. Therein lay the danger. She had deceived him, she was pregnant, and he must never find out.

"I called you Sunday night at eleven, just as I said I would." Adam cupped her chin in his hand, forcing her to look at him. "When I got your brother's answering machine, I thought I'd dialed the wrong number."

He didn't conceal the hurt in his eyes, and Shay's lips quivered.

"I called twice more, then finally looked up your brother's address in the phone book, only to find it was the very apartment where we had spent the weekend."

"Adam, I wish I could explain." She really did, but, of course, she didn't dare.

"I looked up every Flynn in the phone directories for the District and suburban Maryland and Virginia. I called quite a few of them, too."

"Oh, Adam!" Shay impulsively twined her arms around his neck and hugged him tightly. "I—I'm sorry if I hurt you. I didn't want to, but—"

"Shay, we had something very special. I know you felt it, too."

"Yes, yes, I did," she blurted out. "I missed you so much, Adam, but it's hopeless."

He cut her off with an urgently demanding kiss. "Of course it's not hopeless." He kissed her again. "I'm hungry for you, Shay. I have to have you."

Four

She felt the same. Just one night, her heart and body coaxed her mind. Just one more time with him. Her hands swept over his long, hard body and she was lost.

His hands closed possessively over the rounded fullness of her breasts, and an urgent whimper escaped from her throat. When his mouth enveloped her nipple, a deep shudder tore through her, and she grasped his head to hold it there. She felt the firm strokes of his tongue and the gentle nip of his teeth and gasped at the erotic mixture of pleasure and pain. Her knee lifted automatically, and her toes curled into the soft, thick quilt. Adam's hand trailed over her leg, rubbing lightly with his fingertips, then scoring gently with his nails. Shay moaned and tried to capture his hand between her thighs.

"Not yet, sweetheart." Adam laughed softly, eluding her with tantalizing ease. "I want to tease you a little bit first, to punish you for what you've put me through." He caressed her with excruciating slowness, making her twist and writhe for more. "I like the little noises you make when you lose control. I love to hear you moan for me."

They kissed again and again, deep, drugging kisses that rendered her mindless. Adam carelessly tossed the purple jersey and tights onto the floor. The orange mini and bra landed at the foot of the bed. Shay eagerly helped Adam out of his own clothes.

"You're lovely, Shay." Adam's eyes were cloudy with passion as his gaze roved over the curvaceous lines of her body.

Shay gazed up at him, dimly aware that she was playing with fire, that she should stop him now and send him out of her life. But she was too caught up in the throes of arousal; the feelings sweeping through her were too enthralling and too wonderful to give up.

"You do like purple, don't you?" he drawled as he removed her silky orchid panties with agonizing slowness.

"It's my favorite color." She nibbled on his shoulder, a deep satisfaction flowing through her as Adam trembled at her touch. There was something thrilling, something powerful in being able to excite this man. She wanted to do more, to touch him as he was touching her, to make him as helpless in her arms as she was in his. She slid her hand along his hair-roughened chest, pausing to trace his navel with her fingertips before continuing boldly downward.

"Oh, no, little witch." Adam caught her hands and shackled them together with his big hand, pulling them above her head. "Tonight I'm the seducer." His other hand cruised slowly over the smooth skin of her abdomen. "Tonight it's my turn to make you go crazy with wanting me." One long finger touched the very core of her, eliciting her breathless moan. "And after I make you tell me how much you want me, I'm going to take you and make it last, long and slow and deep, until you're—"

A sudden impatient pounding on the front door, accompanied by the equally insistent ringing of the doorbell, caused them both to leap up in alarm.

"Miss Flynn, Miss Flynn!" A chorus of young voices joined the cacophony of knocks and rings. "Are you there, Miss Flynn?"

"What's going on?" Adam seemed dazed, but Shay was instantly fully alert.

"It sounds like some of the kids from school." She frantically grabbed her lilac quilted robe from its hook on the back of the bedroom door. "I'm an art teacher at Carver High," she hastened to explain, suddenly painfully aware of her shocking state of undress. And Adam's as well.

"Well, get rid of them," Adam ordered, and Shay flushed hotly.

"Please, Adam, stay in here. I—I don't want them to think, to—to know—"

Adam sat up, frowning. "If they aren't gone within five minutes, I'm coming out, Shay," he warned, but she had already rushed out of the room.

"Chandra! Tiana! Darlene!" She was surprised to see the three students when she flung open the door. "What are you—"

"Look, Miss Flynn!" Chandra interrupted impatiently, lifting the lid of the battered picnic basket that Tiana and Darlene clutched between them. Inside three kittens nestled together within the folds of a striped flannel blanket.

"Miss Flynn, it was the most awful thing," Darlene cried. "This mean old lady was going to drown them!"

"We told her we'd find homes for them," Tiana inserted. "We couldn't let the old bat kill 'em."

Shay stared from the sleeping kittens to the concerned young faces, all the while excruciatingly aware of Adam's presence in her bedroom. The thought of her students' discovering a man in her apartment, with her dressed only in a robe, was intolerable to her. The questions, the knowing glances, the gossip at school . . . Shay shuddered. It wasn't that the girls must be shielded from the truth; they were already street-smart and too knowledgeable about such matters in the first place. But Shay knew they had a special respect for her, and she didn't want that sullied in any way.

"Hey, Miss Flynn, your hair is baaaad!" Darlene complimented enthusiastically. "I never saw you wear it that way before."

"You going out tonight, Miss Flynn?" Tiana asked with evident interest. "Your eye makeup is bad, too."

"N-no, I—I was just experimenting for a—a play," Shay stammered. Now, why had she said that? It was certainly not immoral for an art teacher to have a date. Pulling nervously at her dreadful rainbow braid, Shay hastened to change the subject.

"Tell me about the kittens, girls. You rescued them from a woman who wanted to drown them?"

"From the old witch who lives in the building across the street from us," Chandra confirmed. "Her cat had them eight weeks ago, and they've already given three away."

"But she couldn't find homes for these and she was going to drown them!" Darlene added indignantly. "We couldn't let her do it, Miss Flynn."

"Of course not," Shay agreed, casting an anxious glance toward her bedroom. If Adam were to come out now . . .

"Our folks wouldn't let us keep them," Tiana said woefully. "Nobody in our building wanted them, and Mr. Deroy is allergic to cats."

"I didn't know that," Shay said in surprise.

"Neither did we," Chandra said. "But as soon as he let us in his apartment with the kittens, he started sneezing."

"Miss Flynn, you're not allergic to cats, are you? Will you take the kittens?" Tiana pleaded.

"Three kittens?" Shay chewed her lower lip, her anxiety mounting by the second. Were the five minutes up? Would Adam carry out his threat and appear? "I'm not sure that this building even allows pets."

"They do," Chandra assured her. "We heard a dog barking as we came up the stairs."

"Yes, of course. That would be Mary Jo's fox terrier. I'd forgotten all about him."

"So pets are allowed. Please, Miss Flynn, won't you take them?" Darlene begged.

In her distracted state, Shay could not summon a case against it. She only wanted to get the girls out of the apartment before Adam put in an appearance. Taking the kittens seemed the quickest way to achieve that goal. Anyway, she'd never had a pet and had always wanted one. Now she would have three.

"I'll need some supplies for them." She rooted through her purse as the girls gave a delighted cheer. "Run down to the store and buy a litter box and some cat food." Handing the ten-dollar bill to Chandra, Shay took the picnic basket and all but pushed the girls out the door. Their excited voices could be heard down the hall until the sound of their footsteps faded away.

"What on earth is going on?"

Shay jumped at the sound of Adam's voice. He was lounging against the door frame of the kitchen, his clothes once again impeccable, his hair carefully combed.

"Who are those children?"

"Three students of mine." Shay found herself unable to meet his steady gaze. "They brought me some kittens."

"Does this happen often?" Adam sounded amused. "Students turning up on your doorstep bearing gifts?"

Shay shrugged. "Sometimes. But this is the first time they've brought anything live." It was difficult to resist returning his smile. "Are you in the market for a cat, by any chance?"

"Sorry." Adam shook his head. "I already have a dog, a black Lab retriever named Bruno, who's used to ruling the roost. You don't really intend to keep them, do you, Shay?"

"I guess so. I love cats, and I've always wanted one."

"But three? Why not contact the ASPCA? I believe

there's an animal shelter not too far from here, and—"

"I want to keep them all," Shay interrupted. "I couldn't pick one and send the others away." She took a deep breath. Adam was dressed; Chandra, Tiana, and Darlene would be back soon. She'd have to do it now. "You'd better leave, Adam," she said as calmly as she could. "The girls will be back any minute and—"

It was Adam's turn to interrupt. "We have a dinner date, Shay."

"Not any more. You've made it clear what you wanted from me tonight, and it wasn't dinner."

"What kind of a remark is that?"

"A crackerjack lawyer like you should be able to figure it out." Shay opened the door and stood pointedly beside it. "I want you to leave now, Adam."

Adam crossed the room to stand in front of her. "Why, Shay? A few minutes ago you were melting in my arms. You wanted me as badly as I wanted you."

"No!" Her face flamed at his blatant words. "You—you forced yourself on me."

"Come on, Shay!" Adam laughed in disbelief. "You know that isn't true."

"It is true!" Her voice rose shrilly. "I didn't want to go out with you tonight, but you insisted. I asked you to leave my apartment earlier and you wouldn't. Then you grabbed me and made me—"

"Shay, stop it!" He stepped toward her, and Shay backed away, thrusting the basket of kittens in front of her like a shield. "Honey, what is it?" Adam's voice softened and took on a soothing quality that she had to force herself to resist. "Are you ashamed of what's happened between us? Are you afraid of your feelings for me? Tell me, and we can talk it out."

"There's nothing to talk about. I'm not ashamed or afraid," she lied. "I'm—I'm just not interested in having an affair with you, Adam. But you seem unable or unwilling to grasp that fact."

Adam sighed heavily. "I'm not into masochism,

Shay. I'm trying hard to understand you, but I don't care for the little games you seem to play compulsively."

"I'm not playing games. I just want you to get out."

"Shay, I find it difficult to stay with a woman who keeps claiming that she wants me to get lost."

"Good. Then perhaps you'll leave?"

His lips curved into a rueful smile. "If you keep this up, I'll begin to believe that you really mean it."

"Believe it, Adam. I don't ever want to see you or hear from you again."

"Shay." He began stroking one of her arms, and she stiffened. "Why are you shutting me out? Why are you pushing me away? You said you missed me, you agreed we had something special—"

Shay took another step back. "I—I was lying."

"I won't do it, Shay," he warned, his temper obviously rising now at an alarming speed. "I won't be dragged into participating in juvenile, neurotic strategies. That sort of thing is useless and destructive. If you tell me to leave again, I'll take you at your word. I'll walk through that door and never contact you again."

She had no choice. She was in danger in his company, saying and feeling and wanting things that she shouldn't. She couldn't trust herself around him. If she were accidentally to blurt out something about the baby . . .

Adam's lips tightened. "The next move is up to you, Shay."

She faced him squarely. "Good-bye, Adam."

He stared at her for one long moment, as if unable to believe that she had called his bluff. Had he actually expected her to pull an about-face and ask him to stay? Did he know how very close she had come to doing just that? What a weak-minded fool she was! Self-contempt shone in her dark blue eyes.

"I don't understand you, Shay," he said hoarsely.

"And you never will!" She flung the words at him. "And I don't care."

Adam clenched his jaw and was gone, without a

word or a backward glance. He was, Shay knew, out of her life forever.

She waited for the flood of relief that should have followed her victory. Instead her heart contracted with pain. She had done the only thing she could, she reminded herself bracingly. Having Adam Prescott Wickwire III in her life, even temporarily, was a complication she couldn't afford. He was dangerous, with his gray eyes that could shine with such warmth and tenderness, his beautiful mouth that— Shay quickly turned her thoughts in another direction.

The kittens. Opening the basket, she gazed down at them, seeing each individually for the first time. There was a black one with four white feet—Spats would be a fitting name for him—a little gray tabby that she'd call Smoky, and a white one with patches of gray and black. Sinclair? The name sprang to mind from nowhere. Why not?

When the girls returned with the supplies, Shay had to force her smile when she told them the kittens' names.

Five

The Arts and Crafts Show at Carver High was a huge success. It had been the best yet, involving more students and a greater selection of artwork and handcrafted items than ever before. The entire inventory had been sold out, and for the first time sales exceeded the thousand-dollar mark. The money was deposited in a special account to be used for the purchase of equipment and supplies. This year a potter's wheel was being considered for the art room.

The following Tuesday Paul Deroy joined Shay and the students in the art room, where an early December tree-trimming party was in progress. As usual, he hadn't come empty-handed, and they helped themselves to the potato chips he offered them. Shay smilingly refused the small bag of chips he handed to her.

Paul gave a mock groan. "If you tell me you've given up junk food, too, I'll put my head in the kiln and turn on the heat. Your nutrition kick is very demoralizing to a snack addict like me, Shay."

Shay sucked in her breath and forced a smile. Paul thought she'd become a health-food fanatic over the past four months. Why didn't she simply tell him that she was watching her diet so carefully because she was pregnant?

It wasn't as easy as she'd once thought it would be, Shay admitted to herself. Although she had kept alive the fiction of a mythical marriage, explaining a sudden reconciliation with her fictional husband and its result was an ordeal she kept postponing. She was still not obviously pregnant, although her waistline had thickened, her breasts were fuller, and her abdomen was no longer flat, but a softly rounded swell.

Shay knew she would be unable to conceal her condition much longer, nor did she want to. She longed to share her wonderful news with the whole world, but . . . Shay sighed. Not today.

"Is the Art Club going caroling this year, Miss Flynn?" Tiana's voice broke into Shay's thoughts.

"Oh yes," Shay answered enthusiastically. "We're scheduled to sing at Children's Hospital the Monday before Christmas. Does that meet with everyone's approval?"

It did.

"Are you and Mr. Deroy going to make out under the mistletoe again this year?" Anthony asked with a smirk.

Shay laughed with the rest of group. The chaste kiss Paul had given her under the mistletoe at last year's Christmas party hardly qualified as "making out," and they all knew it. She met Paul's eyes and quickly looked away when she read the undisguised longing in them. Perhaps even a chaste kiss would be a mistake this year.

Shay picked up a pizza for dinner that evening and was greeted noisily by the kittens, who demanded a share of the pepperoni and anchovies while she ate. The trio's antics never ceased to amuse her. Even when she fell into a melancholy mood, as she often did these days, the kittens could cheer her up and make her laugh.

She blamed the hormonal changes of pregnancy for the uncharacteristic blue funks that had been making her weepy and overemotional. That her thoughts inevitably drifted to Adam Wickwire during those moments was a coincidence she didn't care to analyze.

Who was he with? What was he doing? Did he ever think of her? It was an exercise in futility, Shay scolded herself, but an odd little lump formed in her throat nonetheless. True to his word, Adam had not called or made any attempt to see her again. Shay reminded herself how glad she was. . . .

The ring of the telephone roused her from her reverie. She answered it at once.

"Shay! How are you, honey?"

Candy. Shay smiled with pleasure. "What have you been up to these days, big sister?"

"The Morrison divorce." Candy groaned. "It's probably the most bitter divorce I've ever handled, and you know I've had some all-out wars."

Shay knew. Her sister had developed and nurtured her reputation as a hard-driving, aggressive divorce lawyer. A bomber. A barracuda. Candy answered to both labels.

"Shay, you are all right, aren't you?" Concern shaded Candy's usual brisk tones. "Are you feeling—"

"I'm feeling fine, Candy," Shay reassured her. Candace would forever see her as a child to be worried over and protected, their ten-year age difference being almost a generational one. Casey, Candy's twin, regarded his baby sister in much the same light. "I've never felt better in my life. I'm healthy as a horse, and I have a wonderful doctor who—"

"I wish to hell you had a wonderful husband as well," Candy broke in grimly. "And you know my views on marriage." She switched to a more cheerful subject, her voice deliberately lightening. "Anyway, the main reason I called is to invite you to the party I'm having on Saturday night. Please come, Shay."

Shay's heart sank. She wasn't one for large parties, and Candy's trendy, sophisticated friends made her uncomfortable. "I sort of had plans for Saturday night, Candy."

"Probably to wash your hair and watch television," Candy sniffed. "Come on, Shay, it'll do you good to get out with other adults for a change. And I've even persuaded our brother to leave the hospital and put in an appearance. You know how rarely he does that! You have to come."

Shay sighed, and Candy took it for an affirmation.

"The party starts at eight, but come any time, hon. See you on Saturday." She hung up quickly, before Shay could come up with a convincing refusal.

She wasn't looking forward to the party, but still she bought her first maternity dress to wear to it. It was a prairie-style tent dress in a dark raspberry color, with long sleeves, a ruffled hem, and a boat neck. She hopefully timed her arrival at Candy's to coincide with her brother's, but there was no sign of Casey's flashy Lambourghini within a block of their sister's town-house condominium. Unwilling to make her entrance alone, Shay walked to the back door that opened into the kitchen and knocked.

The caterers let her in. They were talkative and friendly and remembered Shay from Candy's last party. She had spent a large part of it in the kitchen discussing recipes with them.

Twenty minutes after her arrival she was still in the kitchen, when Candy came in, chic and lovely in an emerald silk designer dress. With her was a dark-haired, well-dressed man whom Shay guessed to be somewhere in his late thirties. He had piercing black eyes and was only a few inches taller than Candy, who was Shay's height.

"I figured I'd find you here, Shay," Candy said as she and her escort skirted the table where Shay was sitting. "I want you to meet David Falk. David, this is the baby sister I've been telling you about. Shay Kathleen Flynn."

Shay and David murmured polite greetings while regarding each other with unabashed curiosity. Was he Candy's latest lover? Shay wondered with interest. Candy didn't believe in suppressing the sexual side of her nature, as she put it, and had indulged in a long string of affairs. But she never allowed any man to break through her impenetrable wall of reserve.

"Isn't she pretty, David?" Candy exclaimed enthusiastically. "And she's talented and creative and intelligent, as well as kind and caring. Why, from the time she was—"

"Candace!" Shay was aghast. What was her sister up to now?

"And she's modest, too!" Candy was obviously undaunted.

Shay stared at the floor, her face scarlet. When she got her sister alone . . .

David began to laugh. "Candace, you're as subtle as an MX missile."

"I thought you two should meet." Candy set her jaw in a stubborn way that Shay knew well. "You both have so much in common. You're both crazy about kids, for one, and—"

Shay forced a smile as she interrupted. "I'm mortified, Mr. Falk. I know what my sister has in mind and I'm sorry you've been dragged into her little scheme."

"Hey, no problem." David grinned. "Candace told me all about your plans for single parenthood. I was curious to meet you."

"Don't be angry, Shay," Candy pleaded. "I'm worried about you. The thought of your going through all this alone . . ."

"I'm not alone," Shay countered. "I have you and Case, and I don't want or need anyone else."

"But Shay—"

"What a crush! Did Candace Flynn invite every attorney in Washington?" The high-pitched female voice belonged to a petite brunette in a sexy red cocktail dress who sauntered into the kitchen. "Why, David Falk! Imagine meeting you here."

"Hello, Paulette," David said smoothly, turning to

greet the woman. "Shay, meet Paulette Wilder, paralegal extraordinaire. All the law firms in town are trying to hire her away from Wickwire, Prescott & Sinclair, including my own, but she claims she won't be pirated."

Paulette flashed a brilliant smile. "If you asked me seriously, David, I might consider it." She turned to greet Shay, but was interrupted by another voice.

"Who wants to pirate Paulette?"

The voice was painfully familiar and Shay sat frozen in her chair as Adam Prescott Wickwire III walked casually into the kitchen.

"Hello, Adam." David seemed relieved to see the other man. "You know Candace, of course." Adam nodded to Candy. "And this is her sister, Shay."

Adam turned, then stared at Shay, thunderstruck. "Candace Flynn's sister? You?"

Shay managed a weak nod.

"I take it you two know each other?" David glanced from Adam to Shay. Neither answered him.

Shay remained motionless, stunned, fervently wishing she were anywhere else. Adam's eyes darkened to a deep steel gray and held hers for a moment before his lips twisted into a sardonic smile. "We know each other very well, David." The inflection in his voice told the others just how well.

"If you'll excuse me, I think it's time for me to leave." Shay rose from her chair, her legs surprisingly shaky.

"Because I arrived?" Adam asked caustically.

"Shay is feeling a little under the weather," Candy hastened to explain. "She's expecting her first baby and—"

"Candy!" Shay cried in horror, instinctively clutching her abdomen. Against her will, her gaze flew to Adam's face, and she read the shock registered there.

"I didn't know that you'd married, Shay." Adam was suddenly quite pale.

"Married? A Flynn?" David chortled. "Not a chance. Shay is an increasingly common contemporary phenomenon, Adam. A single mother by choice. She chose a stranger, albeit a carefully researched one, to father her child."

How dare he so blithely reveal the circumstances of her pregnancy! Shay thought wildly. And how much had Candy told David Falk?

"When did she commision this—this stranger?" His complexion had turned a deepening crimson.

"The perfect stranger?" David grinned. He seemed to regard the whole idea as a tremendous joke. "When, Shay? The end of August? That would be about right, since she's almost four months pregnant now."

"I—I'm going home," Shay scarcely recognized her own voice as the kitchen turned a complete somersault before her eyes. She attempted to draw one unsteady breath before her knees buckled and she fainted for the first time in her life.

"Poor Shay! Oh, I wish Case were here."

The distraught tones of her sister's voice penetrated the thick fog enshrouding Shay's brain. Gingerly opening one eye a crack, she could see Candy standing above her, David Falk at her side. They were in Candy's upstairs bedroom and she was lying on her sister's bed.

There was a third person beside the bed, one who remained stonily silent, watching her closely with gunmetal gray eyes. When Shay saw him she longed to faint again. He knew! She could tell by the fury in his eyes. Adam Wickwire knew he was the father of her unborn child.

"I'm taking you home," he said in a low, taut voice when he saw she was awake. "Now."

Shay shivered. "No!" Tears flooded her eyes, and she stifled the urge to sob aloud. What was going to happen now? Her baby, her precious baby . . . Her hand moved to the soft swell of her abdomen and rested protectively there. She heard Adam's sharp intake of breath.

"When is it due, Shay?" His voice was cutting, hostile, the voice of a warring defense lawyer grilling the prosecution's star witness.

"May," she murmured, turning her face to the wall.

"Shay, oh, honey, are you all right?" Candy sank onto the edge of the bed and laid her hand on Shay's forehead. "This is all my fault. I shouldn't have insisted that you come to the party."

"You're not to blame," Adam said grimly. "The fault is completely mine."

"I'm afraid I don't understand." Candy eyed him warily. "Perhaps you'd better leave now. I appreciate your carrying Shay up here, but this really is none of your concern."

"Isn't it?" Adam growled. "I happen to be the father of your sister's child, the perfect stranger she researched so carefully." His voice deepened on a note of rage. "The man she used like a damn stud!"

Shay made a small, strangled sound and rolled onto her stomach, burying her face in the pillow. Candy jumped to her feet. "Good Lord, it can't be!"

"Ask your sister." Adam took Candy's place on the bed and grasped Shay's shoulders, turning her over to face him. "Tell her it's true, Shay. I'm the father of the child you're carrying."

Shay wanted to deny it. Every instinct clamored for her to blurt out a lie, but the words wouldn't come.

"That weekend. You wanted more than to lose your virginity, didn't you?" His grip on her tightened. "You wanted me to make you pregnant."

"Shay, is Adam the father?" David asked gently. "If he is, he has a right to know."

Shay sat up, wrenching free of Adam's grasp. "Yes!" She faced them defiantly, wiping the tears from her cheek with the back of her hand in an unconsciously endearing gesture. "He's the father. But he was never supposed to know."

"It all fits now," Adam said in a low voice. "Your carefully executed disappearance, your determination to keep me out of your life. Shay, how could you do this?"

"Don't put all the blame on her!" Candy snapped. "A woman doesn't get pregnant by herself, Wickwire."

"Candace, why don't we rejoin the party and let Adam and Shay thrash things out between them?" David suggested. "Er—I meant that figuratively, of course."

"To hell with the party," Candy said harshly. "My little sister's welfare is at stake, and I'm not leaving this room until Wickwire offers some sort of monetary support."

"You're planning the paternity suit already, aren't you, counselor?" Adam gritted. "That greedy little brain of yours is computing figures like a cash register."

"I intend to act in the best interests of my sister and her child. This baby is entitled to its father's support until it reaches its majority," Candy replied coldly.

"On that issue, we're in complete accord, Ms. Flynn. I have every intention of supporting my child."

Candy was clearly taken aback. "You do?"

"It's not necessary." Shay finally found her voice, emerging at last from the horrified daze that had blanketed her senses. "I can support my baby myself. In fact, I fully intend to." She directed her remarks to Candy and David, still too frightened to risk a glance at Adam. "I won't accept a dime from him."

"Oh, but you will." Adam spoke before Candy could voice any protest. "I have no intention of allowing my child to be raised in a hovel slightly above the poverty line. Not a Wickwire." He lifted his chin proudly. "My child will be raised with all the priveleges and responsibilities that being a member of my family entails."

"Noblesse oblige." Candy snorted, but her fury seemed to have abated. "An out-of-court settlement will certainly be easier on all concerned."

"This baby is mine. All mine!" Shay cried, panic welling within her. She knew how forceful Candy could be; Adam seemed even more driving. She felt everything was being swept out of her control by the strange alliance between Adam and her sister. "There won't be any settlement at all, either in or out of court. And—and I don't live in a hovel!" She appealed to David, who seemed to be regarding her sympathetically. "Outward appearances don't matter anyway. I'm going to raise my child in a loving, secure environment, and I—"

"I doubt if you know the meaning of that," Adam broke in coolly. "But *our* child will. The baby is going to be raised in my home, Shay, and you're going to marry me as soon as possible. No child of mine will be born illegitimately."

"Marry?" Shay and Candy gasped in unison.

"No, never!" Shay added.

"I must say that's unexpectedly generous of you, Wickwire," Candy said at the same time. "Paying child support is one thing, but to marry—"

"Candy, stay out of this!" Shay had never spoken so fiercely or so furiously to her older sister. Candy's mouth closed in astonishment. "I won't marry you, Adam Wickwire." Shay stood up and clutched at the nightstand for support, her legs trembling so violently she feared she might fall. "I won't sentence my child to the poisonous atmosphere of a marriage of hate."

"Shay, no one is saying that you have to stay married," Candy pointed out. "After the baby is born, I'm sure we can work out an amicable divorce, agreeable to all parties concerned."

"Aren't we jumping the gun by discussing divorce? Shay hasn't even agreed to the marriage yet," David interjected reasonably.

"And I never will!" Shay cried.

"Oh, yes, lady. Yes, you will." Adam rose from the bed and stood directly in front of her, so close she could feel the heat emanating from his hard body. The aromatic mixture of soap and after-shave lotion assailed her nostrils, bringing back sudden, unwanted memories of the other times she had been close to him. So very close.

Shay trembled at the sensual unleashing of those memories and forced herself to concentrate on something else. The tasteful, conservative stripes on his dark brown tie would do.

"There is no way you can make me marry you, Adam." Her voice wavered, and she cleared her throat, determined to sound as forceful as he.

"No?" Adam moved a step closer, so that his solid thighs brushed against hers. "Suppose I take you to court, Shay? It should make an interesting custody case, hmm? Father fights the woman who duped him for their unborn child. And you needn't think that you would automatically win because you are the mother. Those days, thankfully, are gone forever."

"You wouldn't do it!" Shay's heart thundered in her ears. "Your pride and your precious reputation would never permit you to go public in a matter like this."

"Your reputation would suffer far worse than mine, Shay. The woman's always does. Furthermore, my career would be virtually unharmed by the publicity, but yours would be destroyed. Teachers of impressionable youngsters must be above reproach. I predict that you would be fired on the spot." He smiled chillingly. "The judge would be choosing between a gainfully employed father and a mother fired from her job for moral reasons. Who do you think he would find the more suitable guardian?"

Shay blanched. "Don't, Adam," she managed in a choked voice. Her chin quivered as she swallowed a boulder-sized lump in her throat. "Why are you making these threats? You don't really want to marry me, you don't want the baby."

"What makes you think I don't want my child?" Adam's voice was grim. He was so near that she could feel his breath on her cheek. "How dare you make such an assumption, Shay?"

"You don't want a child by me," Shay tried again weakly.

Something flared in his eyes, and his expression was suddenly enigmatic. "I want our child, Shay."

Shay swallowed back a sob of pure misery. She had never planned for him to know he was a father. Had she instinctively known he would want to claim his child?

"I've always wanted children," Adam continued quietly. "Had you researched my first marriage and divorce more carefully, you would have learned that children were a major bone of contention between us. I wanted a family; she didn't."

"The baby is mine," Shay whispered.

"And mine." His voice was suddenly, unexpectedly eager. "My parents and grandparents will be thrilled. They've been hinting, both subtly and broadly, to my sister and me for years to begin the next generation of Prescott-Wickwires."

"Dynastic delusions of grandeur," Candy inserted caustically. "The kid will be part Flynn, too, buster."

Adam ignored her and suddenly smiled down at Shay. "How does this sound? Adam Prescott Wickwire the Fourth. Or perhaps it will be little Miss Prescott Sinclair Wickwire."

"Adam Prescott the Fourth? Prescott Sinclair?" Shay gasped. "I've already chosen the names for my baby. For a boy, Brandon Chad. For a girl, Heather Nicole."

"Forget it." Adam dismissed her choices with a scowl. "The Wickwires are named for family, for tradition. We don't indulge in faddish, trendy names."

"I've chosen beautiful names for my baby! And if you think I'll allow my child to be called anything as pretentious as Adam the Fourth or—or Prescott Sinclair, you're in for a real surprise."

"It sounds as if you two are married already." Candy was amused now. "I think I'm superfluous at this point, so I'll rejoin my guests downstairs while you two talk things out. David?" She extended her arm, and David linked his through it as they left the room.

Adam glared after them. "Exactly what is your relationship with David Falk, Shay?"

"He's a friend," Shay flung back, not bothering to add that she had met him for the first time tonight. "What is your relationship to the paralegal extraordinaire whom everyone wants to pirate?" She regretted the question the moment she'd asked it. "Not that I care," she added hotly.

Adam arched his brow. "I brought Paulette to this party on her own request. She's been stalking your friend Falk for months."

Shay snorted and started to walk away from him, but he caught her round the waist and hauled her against him. "When will you marry me, Shay?" he murmured almost coaxingly.

"Try never!" Shay struggled futilely to free herself. "I don't believe in marriage."

"Well, it's time you did, lady, because you're going to marry me. I intend to see you safely through this pregnancy, Shay."

"How noble! Don't pretend that you give a damn about me, Adam Wickwire. You haven't even bothered to call me once in the past two months."

"You can hardly blame me for that." His arms tightened about her, and even through her anger, Shay felt a bolt of desire shoot through as her soft, full breasts were pressed against his solid chest. "You made it extremely clear that you didn't want me in your life."

"Which you used as a convenient out. Don't try to turn the tables on me, Adam. I'm well acquainted with clever legal sophistry."

For a moment Adam stared at her, nonplussed. "Just what are you trying to say? That you expected me to pursue you after you'd insisted that you wanted nothing to do with me? Did you want to tell me about the baby, Shay?"

Did she? Had she? Shay's mind spun. "You're confusing me."

"Answer the question, Shay."

"Yes—No!" She started to struggle again. "You're trying to trick me!"

"You're irrational." Adam lifted a hand to cup her cheek. "And you're making me as crazy as you are." His eyes blazed with an intensity she knew well. When his head descended, Shay was fully aware of what was coming next.

His mouth closed over hers in a deeply sensuous kiss that made her feel weak and soft and robbed her of all inclination to fight. Adam's hand slid from her cheek to tug at her prim chignon, and her hair tumbled down around her shoulders. "Do you know how hard it's been for me to keep away from you, Shay?"

Shay shook her head slowly, still dazed by the kiss she'd thought she'd never know again.

Adam sat down on the bed, pulling her onto his lap. "I've wanted you so badly. We could have been, should have been, having the most deeply fulfilling, mutually satisfying affair that—"

Affair! She reacted with instant fury, not bothering to analyze the cause of her rage. "I wouldn't have an affair with you if you were the last man on earth!" She tried to pry his hands apart, but they remained shackled around her, imprisoning her on his lap.

"Not very original, honey." Adam nuzzled her neck. "Let's hope the baby inherits my gift of language." One of his hands moved upward to close warmly over her breast. "Yes, your body has changed, hasn't it? I want to see, Shay."

She felt his fingers on the top of the zipper at the back of her dress. "Adam, no!" Her breath caught in her throat as he lowered the zipper to her waist. "Someone might walk in."

"Then they'll see me making love to my wife," Adam said huskily. He shoved the dress off her shoulders, then pulled her arms out of the sleeves, baring her to the waist. "You are almost my wife, Shay," he added, pushing her back against the pillows.

Shay sought frantically to divert him. "This isn't exactly in keeping with your image, Adam." A well-directed conversational offensive had cooled many a man's ardor. "A blue-blooded Virginia gentleman doesn't disappear into the bedroom during a party with a woman who's not even his date for the evening."

"Nothing about my relationship with you conforms to my so-called image," Adam said unconcernedly as he settled himself over her, fitting the hard planes of his body to the soft curves of hers. "I can hardly be blamed for acting out of character." He nibbled a path from her shoulder to the hollow of her throat. "I like your perfume." His voice had a tiny catch in it. "It's a scent I only associate with you. What is it?"

"It's not perfume," she replied breathlessly. "It's just a lilac-scented soap I use." She was becoming increasingly aware of Adam's full warm weight as she continued to struggle halfheartedly beneath him. She felt strangely weak, and a peculiar lethargy flowed through her veins, lessening the urge to fight or even to talk. His lips brushed the sensitive skin of her neck as his fingers dipped inside her bra and touched her nipple, which was already beginning to bud. Shay closed her eyes, involuntarily responding to the exciting warmth stirring deep within her.

Neither was aware of the bedroom door opening, but both heard the startled gasp from the astonished intruder. Adam sat up at once.

"Oh, I'm so sorry!" Paulette Wilder's high, girlish voice fractured the momentary silence. "I didn't mean to interrupt. I—I didn't realize. I'll just go back downstairs and—"

"No, wait a minute, Paulette." Adam stood up and walked over to her.

Shay struggled with the bodice of her dress, miserably embarrassed by her state of undress. Paulette Wilder had certainly gotten an eyeful when she'd walked through that door.

"Paulette, I'm sorry you—er—had to witness this little scene. I'm afraid that Shay and I both got a bit carried away." Adam's voice faltered slightly. "You see, we've finally—ah—settled some long-standing differences between us and have decided to marry. As soon as possible."

"Marry?" Paulette echoed incredulously.

"Adam, don't," Shay warned. "We're not—"

"I know you wanted to be the first to break the news, darling," Adam interrupted, a menacing glimmer in his eyes. "But I did want to explain to Paulette, as she was, er, my date to this affair."

"Congratulations, Adam," Paulette replied in a perfunctory tone. "Oh, why can't it happen that way between David and me? He's scarcely glanced in my direction all evening!" She suddenly dissolved into tears. "It's hopeless, Adam. And I want him so much!"

Adam placed an awkward arm around Paulette's shoulders, looking uncomfortable. Shay scrambled from the bed and zipped her dress with shaking fingers. An opportunity to escape had presented itself, and she had no intention of letting it slip away.

"I think Paulette has suffered enough for one evening, Adam." Shay stumbled to the door. "She needs your full support at a time like this, so I'll just leave you two alone and go home. Right now."

"Come back here, Shay," Adam ordered, but she was already out the door and he was too entangled with Paulette to pursue her. "Shay." His voice followed her into the hall. "I'll be at your apartment at ten tomorrow morning to finish discussing our marriage plans."

As far as Shay was concerned, the discussion was already finished. There were no marriage plans because there would be no marriage.

Safely back in her apartment, Shay fed the kittens and prepared for bed. By tomorrow Adam no doubt would have come to his senses and abandoned the foolhardy notion of marrying her. Shay was so certain of her supposition that she fell into a deep, dreamless sleep almost as soon as she climbed into bed. Snuggled under the quilt, she didn't stir until the ring of the doorbell jarred her awake at ten the next morning.

Six

Groggily Shay pulled on her lilac quilted robe and staggered to the door. A quick glance through the peephole sent her stomach plummeting. It was Adam. He was dressed as conservatively and immaculately as always, in an elegantly Italian-cut, charcoal-gray suit, yellow shirt, and rep tie. His expression was grim. She hesitantly opened the door.

"Not dressed yet?" Adam frowned. "I told you I would be here at ten."

"I was asleep." Shay fumbled with the buttons of her robe, flushing as he looked her over from head to foot. Her hair tumbled over her shoulders to the small of her back, tousled and tangled. Standing next to the fastidiously groomed Adam made her feel awkward and unkempt, and at a definite disadvantage.

"I'll get dressed," she mumbled, heading for the bedroom.

Adam followed her. "I'll choose your dress myself. You're not going to spring one of your costumes on me again."

"I'm not wearing a dress," she said, stopping to greet her kittens, who were lined up by their food bowls. "I'm wearing jeans." She had an oversized pair that fit comfortably.

"Shay, I realize that I'm probably too much of a traditionalist, but I want my bride to wear a dress for our wedding. Not jeans."

Shay straightened abruptly. "Wedding?" She felt her heart stop, then start again. "T-today?"

"Why not? There's a place in Fairfax that condenses the usual three-day waiting period for a blood test and license into a few hours. It sounds tailor-made for a situation such as ours."

"Adam, be reasonable!" She stalked into her bedroom. "There is no need for us to get married!"

"There is every need, Shay. In five months you'll be giving birth to my child." He went directly to her closet and opened it. "I've never shirked my responsibilities, and you and the baby are most definitely—" He broke off, his tone changing to one of disbelief. "This can't be your entire wardrobe! You must have something more suitable than what's in here."

"My wardrobe is quite suitable for my needs. It doesn't include what you would consider an appropriate wedding dress because I have no need to get married. I'm never going to marry!"

"I don't think you know what you want—or what you need, Shay." Adam removed the dark raspberry dress she had worn the night before and surveyed it critically. "I guess this one will have to do. I can see that I'll be spending a fortune on clothes for you in those chic maternity boutiques."

He handed her the dress, and she promptly flung it down on the unmade bed.

Adam folded his arms across his chest. "Shay, I'm trying hard not to lose patience with you. I know you're upset and confused." His voice softened. "Just let me make the decision for you, honey. Remember, we have a child to consider, an innocent baby who deserves to be born legitimately."

"Is that so important?" Shay cried. Adam certainly seemed to think so; Candy, too. But maybe that was because they were both lawyers, who liked everything legal and tidy . . . and legitimate. Desperately she tried another tack. "Ann Landers says that a child is better off in a loving one-parent home than in—"

"We haven't time to write to Ann," Adam cut in, "but I'm sure she would agree that a child should be spared the stigma of illegitimacy. And it is still a stigma, Shay. Even in these so-called enlightened times."

"Particularly for a Wickwire," Shay shot back.

"For anyone, Shay."

She glared at him. Lawyers were never without a comeback. She'd learned that from observing her sister. They seemed to possess an inexhaustible supply of ready comments.

"I talked to your brother at the party last night, Shay."

A switch in subjects. Another tactic, Shay thought sourly.

"He's concerned about you, Shay. He agrees that marriage is the right solution."

"For two committed singles, Case and Candy are certainly freely prescribing marriage for me," Shay said dryly. "Well, I won't— What—what are you doing?" she gasped as Adam began to unfasten her robe.

"Undressing you," he replied calmly, slipping the robe from her shoulders. Underneath it Shay was wearing an oversized white nightshirt with dark purple stripes on the sleeves and a large purple twelve on the front.

"When people ask what to give as wedding gifts, I'll suggest lingerie," Adam said wryly. "For your benefit as well as mine."

Shay flushed scarlet at the implication and grabbed for her robe. Adam held it just out of her reach.

"Go to hell, Adam Wickwire!" she spat furiously.

"Marrying you, I fear that's exactly where I'm headed."

"Well, since you feel that way about it, why don't we just skip the wedding and—"

"We've done enough sparring on the subject, Shay," Adam interrupted wearily. "If you aren't dressed and ready to leave in fifteen minutes, I'll assume that you intend to fight me on legal grounds for the custody of the baby and I'll proceed accordingly. A few phone calls should start the judicial wheels turning." He left the bedroom, quietly closing the door behind him.

Sick with anxiety, Shay stared unblinkingly at the door, then shakily removed her nightshirt. She was confused, her mind swirling with incoherent half-thoughts that all led to the same dreadful conclusion. If she didn't marry Adam, he would take her baby from her. She didn't dare chance that he might be bluffing. Candy had told her many times that any lawyer worth his degree was prepared to back up threats with action. Candy never made idle threats; Shay doubted that Adam Wickwire did either.

She dressed in a daze, brushing and braiding her hair with unsteady fingers. To bring her baby into the world and be immediately plunged into a custody fight . . . one that she stood every chance of losing . . .

Her thick sable braid hung down her back, nearly to her waist, and she applied a minimum of makeup. Her face was very pale.

"Hardly a radiant bride," was Adam's only comment as she emerged from the bedroom.

"Hardly," she agreed coldly. "I'll get my coat."

As she opened the door of the front closet, a gray ball of fur streaked between her ankles to attack the boots on the closet floor. He was followed seconds later by two more mewing fur bundles.

"The cats are going to be a problem." Adam frowned watching them. "Neither my housekeeper nor my dog will tolerate having three cats in the house."

"You don't expect me to move into your house?"

Shay was appalled. Having barely consented to the marriage, the prospect of moving in with Adam was too outlandish to be considered. "Why, it's out of the question! For one thing, I'd be miles farther from work, and the commute would be horrendous. As for giving up my kittens to please your housekeeper, not a chance! We're staying here."

"You will move into my home, Shay. Husbands and wives generally do share the same residence, particularly as newlyweds."

"You can't have everything your way, Adam Wickwire." Shay folded her arms in front of her chest and regarded him mutinously. "With your threats you might bully me into marrying you, but I refuse to part with my cats. They're the first and only pets I've ever had and I—I love them. And they love me, too!"

Adam stared at her for a long moment, then sighed. "If I agree to having the cats, will you move into my house without further argument?"

Realizing she had won a victory of sorts, Shay nodded. Lawyers were great bargainers, she recalled. Candy was continuously trading off one thing for another in her divorce cases.

"You needn't look so pleased with yourself," Adam grumbled. "Maria will probably quit when those three felines invade her turf. She barely tolerates Bruno."

"Who's Maria? Your housekeeper?"

Adam nodded. "She's a marvel. Certain neighbors have been trying to hire her away for years. If she leaves, Shay, you can be expected to fill the position."

"What a chauvinistic attitude! If she quits we can both do the housework."

That seemed to silence him effectively. Not one word was exchanged during the short drive into Virginia. Only the melodious strains of a piano concerto from the car's built-in cassette player covered the heavy, tense silence. Shay stared out the window of the elegant silver-gray Mercedes and wished she were in her old Buick listening to Willie Nelson on the radio.

"We're here," Adam announced unnecessarily as he swung the car into a parking lot adjacent to a tall office building. Shay felt an almost overwhelming urge to leap from the car and run away. They walked in silence to the entrance of the building, Shay lagging slightly behind.

"You look like you're walking the Last Mile." Adam's lips quirked as he guided her to a set of elevators inside. Shay made no comment, and the brief elevator ride was completed in glum silence. The doors snapped open, and they stepped out.

"Oh, no!" Adam's low groan instantly commanded her attention.

She followed his gaze to the handsome, dark-suited man emerging from one of the offices along the corridor.

"Tripp!" The man spotted Adam and crossed the hall, extending his hand with a wide grin.

Shay stared from Adam to the other man as they shook hands. Tripp?

"Van, good to see you."

Shay detected the forced note in Adam's attempt at heartiness. She studied the newcomer, observing his expensive attire—suit, shirt, tie, shoes, gold watch. He might have been Adam's clone, and she was not surprised when Adam introduced him as "William Van Horne, who was with me at Andover."

Van dismissed Shay in a glance. It was obvious she was not one of them, no doubt an employee or *pro bono publico* client. "What are you doing here, Adam?" Van's hazel eyes flashed with sudden inspiration. "Getting married, huh?" He slapped Adam on the back, overcome with his own wit.

Shay watched the dark flush stain Adam's cheeks, watched him swallow and draw himself to his full height, at least an inch or two taller than the roaring Van. "Yes, as a matter of fact I—we are." He moved fractionally away from Van to take Shay's hand. "Aren't we, darling?"

The expression on William Van Horne's face was

comical; under other circumstances, Shay would have laughed aloud.

"You are?" The man was obviously stunned, unflatteringly so. "Well, well, well. Er—what's her name again?"

"Shay Flynn," Shay replied coolly. "Candace Flynn's sister."

"Well, well," Van repeated in an enthusiastic, entirely false tone. "This is a real surprise, Tripp. I was at the club on Thursday, and no one mentioned a word about it."

"They didn't know," Shay offered helpfully. "It's been very sudden. A shotgun wedding."

"She's got a great sense of humor, I can see that." Van laughed, backing slightly away. "So, when is the big day?"

"Today." Adam abandoned all attempts at heartiness, enthusiasm, and humor. "Van, I'd appreciate it if you didn't say anything until Monday, at the earliest. I want to tell my family first and—"

"Does Bunny know?" Van whispered in an aside not meant to be heard by Shay.

She heard it. "*Does* Bunny know, darling?" she asked sweetly.

Adam glared at Van, who regarded him with real sympathy. "I won't say a word to anyone, Tripp, you can count on me. Listen, I've got to run. Let's meet for lunch next week, play some squash, hmmm?" Van was backing down the hall as he spoke, obviously eager to escape. They watched him disappear into an elevator.

"Who," Shay asked in icicle tones, "is Bunny?"

"Porter Sloan Warrington, originally of Greenwich, Connecticut, currently residing in Washington. She's a junior associate with Wickwire, Prescott & Sinclair. Any other questions?"

"No." The name said it all. Porter Sloan "Bunny" Warrington. The female version of Adam himself: old family, old money, prep school, Ivy League education. A woman from his own world, which she, Shay Flynn, daughter of a compulsive gambler and frustrated dime-store clerk, clearly was not.

"I just hope Van will keep his mouth shut." Adam was scowling. "His mother is a good friend of my mother's. I'd hate for her to hear the news from Helen Van Horne."

"It will be a nasty shock no matter who tells her. Adam Prescott Wickwire the Third marrying a nobody—a pregnant nobody," Shay amended succinctly. "And what about your friend Bunny? How will she react to the news?"

"I don't think she'll be too pleased," Adam said dryly. "She's made no secret of the fact that she has hopes for the two of us in the future."

"Is she in love with you?" Shay asked, a curious tightness in her chest. "Do you love her?"

"Love," Adam scoffed. "I'm thirty-six years old, Shay, and Bunny is thirty. We're hardly a pair of starry-eyed adolescents caught up in the illusion of romantic love. Bunny was my sister's college roommate. She knows my family well, and we have similar backgrounds and interests. I suppose it was logical to assume that we might have had a comfortable marriage someday, although I was certainly in no rush to marry her. And vice versa."

"Are all members of the privileged set so dispassionate about love and marriage?" She was strangely elated by Adam's apathy toward the other woman. "No wonder their birth rate is steadily declining."

"Well, I'm not dispassionate about my marriage to you, Miss Flynn," Adam retorted. "And we've already done our part to bolster the birth rate."

Shay quickly changed the subject. "Why does Van call you Tripp?"

"It's an old nickname of mine."

"Ah, like Bunny. From prep school, no doubt?"

"No, actually, my family started it. Since I'm Adam the Third, they—"

"I see," she interrupted. "Tripp for triple or three or

tertiary or third. That's interesting. What would they nickname Adam the Fourth? Quad?"

She thought she detected a gleam of humor in his eyes, but he didn't succumb to it. He took her arm and pulled her along the corridor with him. "Come on, Shay. We may as well get this over with."

A sentiment similar to one facing a root canal, Shay thought several times during the next few hours. When they emerged at last from the building, as Mr. and Mrs. Adam Prescott Wickwire III, she was hungry, exhausted, and thoroughly depressed. She allowed Adam to lead her back to the car, too dispirited even to try to pull her hand from his. Adam maintained the grimly sober mien that had been his throughout the long routine of blood work, paper work, and, finally, the brief civil ceremony itself.

"It's close to five o'clock." Adam glanced at his watch as Shay stared silently ahead. Her brain seemed to have short-circuited. Only one thought tumbled through her mind in endless refrain. She was married. Married! It was cruel irony that she was caught in the same miserable trap as her parents before her—and despite her vows to avoid it.

"Why don't we stop at a restaurant for an early dinner?" Adam continued, and she forced herself to listen. "I don't know about you, but I'm starved. Those cheese sandwiches from the vending machines did nothing to appease my appetite."

"It wasn't even cheese," Shay intoned gloomily. "It was processed cheese food."

"Despicable stuff," Adam agreed. "Where would you like to eat?"

Shay shrugged her indifference.

"We never did make it to the Lion d'Or." His reference to their aborted dinner date brought back sharp memories of how they had spent part of that evening. Shay blushed hotly.

"Would you like to go there tonight? We won't need a reservation, since we're unfashionably early." Adam smiled slightly. "We can pretend we're tourists."

"There's no need for me to pretend to be anything other than what I am." Shay tilted her chin proudly. "I've always been unfashionable and I don't care!"

To her consternation, Adam laughed. "You are unique, Shay. I never know what you'll say or do next. Most women would have heart palpitations if someone accused them of being unfashionable. But you boast about it!" He laughed harder. "At least life with you will never be dull."

"Oh, it won't be dull. States of war never are."

There were two other couples in the dimly lit restaurant, both obviously out-of-towners. The maitre d' greeted Adam by name and did a masterful job of concealing his surprise at a Wickwire's appearance at this unfashionable, touristy hour.

"Have you ever eaten here before, Shay?" Adam asked in an irritatingly patronizing tone that implied that she had not. He probably thought that dining out to her meant McDonald's.

"Yes, I have," she replied coolly. "I often go out to dinner with Case and Candy, so you needn't worry that I'll eat the soup with a fork or bathe in the finger bowl."

"There's no need to be so defensive, Shay. I was merely asking. Would you like a cocktail before dinner?" he persevered, the epitome of politeness.

Shay felt churlish and outclassed. She forced herself to reply in a pleasantly neutral tone, "No, thank you. My doctor told me to stay away from alcohol during my pregnancy."

"I see. Do you mind if I have a drink?"

"Of course not."

Adam ordered a double Scotch on the rocks and downed it in three swallows. Shay hid a smile. "It's been that kind of a day, huh?"

The polite tone was set, and for the remainder of the meal both observed the uneasy truce. Shay was surprised to find herself ravenous—usually her appetite was the first thing to go in times of stress—and she consumed the stuffed loin of veal, rice pilaf, and sautéed broccoli, cauliflower, and carrots with gusto.

"Dessert?" Adam asked as the waiter cleared the table.

Shay promptly ordered the chocolate mousse.

"That was delicious," she commented as she finished the last spoonful. The meal had revived her flagging spirits remarkably.

"It's still rather early." Adam cast a quick glance at his watch. "Is there anywhere in particular you would care to go?"

"I'd like to go back to my apartment and paint." Shay sighed. "Sally Vasey had a few extra orders for me to be filled before Christmas." She thought wistfully of the quiet day she had originally planned, painting Christmas designs on needlepoint canvases. Instead she had wasted the entire day at a marriage mill . . . getting married!

"This isn't exactly what I'd planned for this weekend either," Adam said defensively, as if divining her thoughts. "I was supposed to go to Ed Stanton's Christmas party tonight—he's one of the junior partners in the firm—and— Oh, no!" His expression changed to one of chagrin. "I forgot to call Bunny and break our date! She's expecting me at seven-thirty."

Shay saw an out and instantly seized it. "Why don't you go to the party, Adam? You can drop me off at my apartment and go on from there to pick up Bunny."

"Go out with another woman on my wedding night?" Adam stared at her, incredulous. "You can't be serious, Shay."

"I am. There's no reason to change our plans simply because a judge read a few words in front of us today."

"Those few words happened to be marriage vows, Shay," he said in a tight voice. "Legally and morally binding. I will not make a mockery of them by dating one woman on the very day I marry another."

Shay toyed with the salt shaker. "You really are stiflingly conservative and conventional, Adam."

"Another flaw in the character of us privileged types." Adam returned dryly. "Unless you want to go to the party with me, we'll drive to my house in Potomac tonight, where we will spend our wedding night together . . . in the traditional way."

Shay felt the color drain from her face. "I'd rather spend the night alone in my apartment, Adam. I'm very tired and—"

"Let me guess, you have a headache. It won't work, Shay. I'm spending the night with my bride. My stiflingly conservative and conventional character insists upon it. Whether we go to the party first doesn't matter to me. The choice is yours."

"Suppose I choose none of the above?" Shay gulped.

"That isn't one of your options, honey." Adam flashed an almost feral smile. "Well, Mrs. Wickwire?"

Seven

Inspiration struck. "I want to go to a movie," Shay announced.

"A movie?" Adam echoed.

"Yes. It's still early, remember? You asked me if there was anything I wanted to do and . . . I want to go to a movie. We can pretend that we're on, uh, a date."

He appeared to be considering her suggestion carefully. "All right," he said after a moment. "We'll go to a movie. What do you want to see?"

"You choose," she offered graciously. Not being much of a movie-goer, she was unsure what was playing at the time.

"You're stalling, Shay. You're no more interested in seeing a movie than I am." Adam walked around the table to assist her out of her chair. The touch of his fingers on her upper arm seemed to scorch her skin, and Shay staggered slightly as he guided her through the restaurant to the door.

Her wild reaction to his touch confirmed her decision. She needed a respite, time to regroup her defenses before spending a "traditional wedding night" with her new husband. "I really would like to see a movie with you, Adam." She appealed to him with wide blue eyes, wondering if she was overdoing it a bit as she fluttered her lashes, à la Scarlett O'Hara.

To her amazement, Adam's resistance seemed to melt. "Oh, well, why not? Have you seen the latest James Bond flick?"

Shay shook her head. She hadn't seen any of the James Bond movies and, until this moment, had never wanted to. She batted her eyes again. "But I'd love to see it, Adam."

Adam seemed thoroughly engrossed in Agent 007's gadgetries and long-legged beauties. Shay's eyes remained fixed on the screen, but she was too intensely aware of the man beside her to concentrate on the escapades of the movie hero.

She covertly studied Adam's profile—the fine, straight nose and strong chin. Her gaze lingered on the sensual fullness of his lower lip and a knot began to pulsate deep within her. As if to restrain her wanton urges, Shay primly folded her hands together and placed them in her lap. If she leaned the slightest degree to the right, her shoulder would brush Adam's arm. If she crossed her legs, her knee would touch his.

She fidgeted restlessly in her seat until Adam casually dropped his hand into her lap and entwined his fingers with hers. The pressure of his hand against her thighs electrified her, and she closed her eyes against the dizzying sensual waves that washed over her.

She wanted to feel the pressure of Adam's mouth on hers, to be caressed into breathless submission by his big, firm hands. The realization horrified her. As his wife, she was already too much in this man's power. If he were to guess at the depths of her physical longing for him, the way her whole body ached for his touch . . .

The lights snapped on in the theater and Shay gazed around dazedly, as if emerging from a trance. There was the hum of voices and the muffled sound of footsteps. The credits were rolling across the screen.

Adam was watching her, amusement lurking in his eyes. "Did you enjoy the movie, Shay?"

"Yes, very much," Shay lied, avoiding his gaze.

Damn it, he knew. She chewed her lower lip in vexation. He knew that she had been too disturbed by his presence to pay attention to the action on the screen. Her vulnerability was all too clear to both of them.

"It's a beautiful night, isn't it?" Adam remarked as they walked to the car. "Clear and crisp. I think I can even see a few stars in the sky."

"You're hallucinating," Shay said dampeningly. "Stars haven't been seen in the D.C. area for years. The air pollution obliterated them from sight."

"Have a heart, Shay. I'm trying to set a mood. This is not the time to bring up air pollution."

His droll smile alarmingly weakened her resolve to remain aloof. "I have to go back to my apartment now, Adam," she announced in an attempt to revive hostilities. "The kittens need to be fed tonight and early in the morning."

The hostilities were not revived. "Fine," Adam said with a nod. "We'll stay at your place tonight."

She hadn't expected him to be so agreeable. How could she keep him at a distance when he refused to argue with her? Shay tried again. "I won't sleep with you tonight, Adam."

"Yes, darling." Adam smiled a wolfish smile, not at all angry. "Oh, yes, you will."

What now? She had thrown down the gauntlet and he hadn't picked it up, he'd ignored it! Shay tried to gather her scattered wits. She ought to be able to launch a quarrel successfully; she'd grown up with a couple of experts in the field.

"I positively refuse to let you make love to me, Adam Wickwire."

"Why, honey?" Adam reached across the seat for her hand and carried it to his lips. "You know you want me to, Shay."

"I don't!"

"Shay, you were practically on fire for me in the movie theater. Did you think I hadn't noticed?"

Her face burned, and she snatched her hand away. "You're arrogant! And crude!"

"You're fighting yourself, Shay. And I'm not sure I understand why."

Shay wasn't sure either. But some driving force within her deemed it imperative to resist this overpoweringly irresistible man. To surrender to her inexplicable need for him was to invite a dependency fraught with danger. Shay had learned early that those you longed to trust weren't always trustworthy; only her sister and brother were safe to love. And her unborn child, of course.

"Darling, you can't possibly feel any guilt about sleeping with me now," Adam said soothingly. Shay knew he was trying to understand her, and marveled at how far off the mark he actually was. She'd never felt a moment's guilt about sleeping with him; it had been so natural, so right.

"We're married, Shay."

"But you never would have considered marrying me if I hadn't been pregnant." Shay's blue eyes flashed defiantly. Why did that knowledge rankle so? "You said yourself that what you wanted from me was an affair. A fulfilling, mutually satisfying affair. Those were your exact words."

"But we didn't have that affair, did we, Shay? I married you instead."

"Much to your regret—and mine!"

"Dammit, Shay. I'd almost forgotten how exasperating you can be," Adam snapped. "You push and push until you've—" His voice broke off. He was visibly restraining himself from saying more; Shay knew it from the knuckle-whitening grip he had on the steering wheel.

Well, she had done it, Shay noted as she huddled against the window. She had successfully provoked him and killed his good humor, just as she had intended to do. So why did she feel so miserable?

The kittens were delighted to see her and Shay spent a long time feeding and petting and playing with them. Adam watched the interaction from the orchid armchair but made no attempt to join in.

"Would you like, uh, some coffee?" Shay finally acknowledged his presence after ignoring it for three-quarters of an hour. The kittens had grown bored with her and retired to their box in the bedroom for a nap.

"No," Adam replied flatly.

Shay perched tentatively on the chair opposite his. "Maybe you'd like to watch TV? I'll turn it on."

"The perfect hostess. So attentive to her guests," Adam mocked. "No, Shay, I don't want to watch television."

"You don't want coffee, you don't want to watch television. You simply want to sit there and glare at me." She glared right back at him.

"Why are you so antimarriage, Shay?" he asked suddenly, sitting forward. "It's not just marriage to me that you're against, it's the institution of marriage itself. I'd like to know why."

She had a ready answer to that question, one she had been formulating all her life. "Marriage is a union of stress and turmoil and tension that has been overly romanticized and falsely sanctified." She paused for breath. "It's a fatal trap, ensnaring its victims and slowly poisoning them until whatever good qualities they once possessed are totally destroyed."

"From where do you draw your observations?" he asked quietly. "Your sister's divorce practice?"

"Partly." She shrugged. "She sees it every day. How marriage transforms people who were once loving,

A Magical World of Enchantment Awaits You When You're Loveswept!

Your heart will be swept away with Loveswept Romances when you meet exciting heroes you'll fall in love with...beautiful heroines you'll identify with. Share the laughter, tears and the passion of unforgettable couples as love works its magic spell. These romances will lift you into the exciting world of love, charm and enchantment!

You'll enjoy award-winning authors such as Iris Johansen, Sandra Brown, Kay Hooper and others who top the best-seller lists. Each offers a kaleidoscope of adventure and passion that will enthrall, excite and exhilarate you with the magic of being Loveswept!

- ♥ *We'd like to send you 6 new novels to enjoy—<u>risk free!</u>*
- ♥ *There's no obligation to buy.*
- ♥ *6 exciting romances—plus your <u>free gift</u>—brought right to your door!*
- ♥ *Convenient money-saving, time-saving home delivery!*

Join the Loveswept at-home reader service and we'll send you 6 new romances about once a month—<u>before they appear in the bookstore!</u> You always get 15 days to preview them before you decide. Keep only those you want. Each book is yours for only $2.25*. That's a total savings of $3.00 off the retail price for each 6 book shipment.

*plus shipping & handling and sales tax in NY and Canada

Enjoy 6 Romances–Risk Free! Plus...
An Exclusive Romance Novel Free!

Detach and mail card today!

Loveswept

AFFIX RISK FREE BOOK STAMP HERE.

Yes! Please send my 6 Loveswept novels RISK FREE along with the exclusive romance novel "Larger Than Life" as my *free gift* to keep.

RA1

412 28

NAME

ADDRESS   APT.

CITY

STATE   ZIP

MY "NO RISK"
Guarantee

I understand when I accept your offer for Loveswept Romances I'll receive the 6 newest Loveswept novels right at home about once a month (before they're in bookstores!). I'll have 15 days to look them over. If I don't like the books, I'll simply return them and owe nothing. You even pay the return postage. Otherwise, I'll pay just $2.25 per book (plus shipping & handling & sales tax in NY and Canada). I *save* $3.00 off the retail price of the 6 books! I understand there's no obligation to buy and I can cancel anytime. No matter what, the gift is mine to keep–*free!*

SEND NO MONEY NOW. Prices subject to change. Orders subject to approval.

rational human beings into bitter, vengeful monsters."

"That's a very unbalanced view, Shay. Candy is a divorce lawyer, one specifically hired by those seeking vengeance. Of course, that's the only side of marriage she sees."

"Is there another?" Shay asked flippantly. "I wouldn't know. My parents' marriage was one of the world's worst—drinking, gambling, adultery, screaming quarrels, and physical abuse on both sides. Having escaped that once, I vowed never to be subjected to it again."

"It can be different, Shay. My parents have been happily married for forty years, my grandparents for over sixty."

"I know." The statistics had boggled her mind. She still found them difficult to comprehend.

"Of course, your research." Adam smiled wryly. "So you see? It can be done."

"Your parents and grandparents are the exception, not the rule. You yourself are proof of that, Adam. Even coming from such an idyllic marital background, your own marriage failed."

"My first marriage," Adam corrected. "And it failed because Caroline and I married for all the wrong reasons. We'd been dating for years. Most of our friends were getting married at the time. Our relationship was superficial, without any real depth. We weren't in love, we were merely a habit with each other."

"Well, your reasons for marrying a second time are even worse! We hardly know each other, we have no mutual friends, our relationship, if you can even call it that, is based solely on—"

"Where are your parents now, Shay?" Adam interrupted.

The abrupt change of topic caught her off guard, making her lose her train of thought. As it was meant to do? Shay wondered, scowling. "My mother is dead. She was killed in a bus accident on her way to work eleven years ago. Afterward I came to live here in Washington with Case and Candy."

"And your father?"

"He and Mother split up when I was twelve. I wish they'd done it years earlier. They hated each other for as long as I can remember." Shay shuddered at the memories of the endless fighting, of the hatred and the fury that had poisoned her childhood. "I haven't seen much of my father since then. He spends his time shuttling between Las Vegas, Atlantic City, and any race track. Anywhere he thinks he can win big money. Of course he never does. Case and Candy hear from him when he desperately needs money, usually when the loan sharks are threatening him."

She managed a bitter smile. "My background is hardly appropriate for a Wickwire, and I never meant to become one. I just wanted—"

"My chromosomes," Adam said dryly. "Tell me, Shay, with your particular obsession with eugenics, why didn't you go to one of those repositories and request a Nobel laureate donor?"

Shay blushed. "I—I didn't want my baby to be something out of *Future Shock*. I, er, wanted to become p-pregnant the natural way."

Adam rolled his eyes heavenward. "There are plenty of genetically appealing men in Washington, Shay. Why didn't you choose a member of Congress or a White House aide? Whatever made you decide on me?"

He was watching her intently, an indecipherable expression on his face. Shay found herself unable to meet his eyes, so she closed her own. He had asked the one question for which she had no answer. She couldn't explain it, not even to herself. How could she tell him of the tremendous impact he'd had on her senses that first time she'd seen him? How did one explain the almost stunning recognition that this man was the one she had been searching for, the one man to be the father of her child?

"You're exhausted."

Shay opened her eyes to see Adam standing above her. "Come to bed, Shay."

"I'm not really tired, Adam," she said, feeling a flutter of panic. "I'll just sit up and watch TV a while."

"Not really tired?" he repeated mockingly, catching her hands and pulling her to her feet. "You can hardly keep your eyes open. Now, will you walk or shall I carry you to bed?"

What had he said earlier? "We'll spend our wedding night in the traditional way." Shay paled. She was too confused and too exhausted to cope with the notion of a determinedly passionate wedding night. "Please, Adam, I can't—I don't . . ."

Adam's smile faded. "If you think I have any inclination to make love to you right now, you vastly overrate your attraction, lady. All I want to do is to fall asleep as soon as my head hits the pillow."

Which is exactly what he did. By the time Shay emerged from the bathroom in a soft, purple flannel nightgown printed with pink roses, her braid lying over one shoulder, Adam was sprawled on the bed on his stomach, sound asleep. She debated whether or not to sleep on the sofa and decided against it. It was only a two-seater, too small and too short to be comfortable. She was groggy with fatigue and badly needed sleep, for herself and the baby. Cautiously Shay slipped into bed and pulled the covers around her. For a few minutes she lay rigidly on her side, hugging the edge of the bed, willing herself not to breathe. But when Adam didn't stir, when his breathing remained deep and slow and even, she began to relax. The kittens jumped up onto the foot of the bed, purring as they settled themselves into the folds of the quilt. Lulled by their rumbling contentment, Shay soon fell into a heavy sleep.

Hours later, still half-asleep, Shay didn't think to question the source of the furnacelike heat that warmed her bed. Drowsily she curled into the warmth and uttered a small sigh of satisfaction. When a large palm deftly stroked along the long, smooth length of her legs, pushing her nightgown up to her hips, her eyes flew open in alarm.

"Adam?" She was curved against him, spoon-fashion, and he inserted a muscular, hair-roughened thigh between hers as his hand continued upward to cup her breast.

"I'm here, sweetheart." His lips were moistly exploring the tender hollow of her neck. His fingers began to gently massage her nipples, and a melting warmth poured through her. Her body was pliant and relaxed from her deep sleep, and she couldn't summon the willpower to move or even speak.

The sensations produced by his stroking fingers were enthralling, and her whole body began to throb with pleasure. "I think we can dispense with this," Adam murmured huskily, removing her nightgown with one quick movement. "I'll keep you warm, little Shay."

She tried to summon a protest, but her mind was spinning and the words were never said. Adam's hands worked their sensual magic as he continued to caress her arousingly, excitingly. He fondled the nape of her neck and the smooth line of her shoulders; he played with her breasts until they seemed to come alive in his hands.

Shay felt lost in an erotic dream. A piercing shaft of desire cut deeply within her as Adam possessively cradled her against his thighs. He wanted her. She was suddenly elated with the knowledge, with the hard physical response he couldn't hide. Her body moved sinuously against his, her movements urgent and instinctive and born out of a primitive need.

When Adam turned her to face him, her mouth met his hungrily, opening for the hot penetration of his tongue. They kissed again and again, deeply, passionately. Shay clung to him, drunk on the taste and the smell and the feel of him. A liquid heaviness filled her lower body, and when he touched her intimately in the erotic caress that had driven her wild once before, she moaned and arched toward his hand, seeking more. Her violent loss of control thrust her back to the brink of sanity. She gazed into his gray eyes, now deep and dark with passion, and felt a thrill of alarm.

"Adam, I don't think—"

"Excellent, my darling." He chuckled softly, tantalizing her with his probing fingers. "Don't think. I don't want you to think at all." His mouth opened over hers, and her eyelids fluttered shut.

She could feel the hammering of his heartbeat against her and was overcome by a sudden, inexplicable wave of tenderness. He wanted her very badly. And it had become oddly important to her to fill that need of his, to give him what he wanted.

"I need you, Shay," he muttered hoarsely, and she nodded dreamily, stroking his hair with gentle fingers. Yes, she knew he needed her in a way no one else ever had. It was an irresistible and alluring notion.

"I want you so much, Shay. I can't ever remember wanting a woman the way I want you." His huskily spoken words completed the seduction begun by his lips and hands. Shay had always wondered if she was somehow lacking, and here was a godlike Adam Wickwire telling her he wanted her more than any other woman. She melted in his arms, surrendering completely.

He eased her over on her back, scrutinizing her intensely. Shay felt no shame in her nakedness; she basked in the heat of his silver stare.

"Your body is no longer the slim, virginal one I first knew," he whispered, moving his hands tenderly over each rounded curve. "Your breasts are fuller, your hips are more rounded, your belly is beginning to swell. You're more beautiful and more desirable than ever before, Shay."

She thrilled to his words. Capturing one hand, which rested on the soft swell of her abdomen, she brought it to her lips and kissed his palm and each

finger in turn. She was aching with the need to give,
and when Adam demanded, "Tell me that you want
me," she complied, unable to refuse him anything.

"I want you, Adam." She hardly recognized the
throaty purr as her own voice. "I want you so much."

With a slight smile of satisfaction, he lay down on
his back. "Ask me to make love to you. Plead with me
not to stop."

Shay was too lost in passion to do anything but
surrender to his commands. Leaning over him, the
tips of her breasts grazing the mat of wiry hair on his
chest, she stroked his cheek and whispered, "Make
love to me, Adam. Please."

"Show me how much you want me." Adam watched
her through narrowed eyes. "The way you did the
night you wanted to become pregnant."

The knowledge she had stored from her lovemak-
ing research, coupled with instincts she didn't know
she had, came readily to the fore. Shay found herself
the aggressor as she pleasured Adam with her lips
and hands. Her technique must have been extremely
effective for Adam suddenly pushed her onto her
back, then moved over her with a hungry groan of
passion. She absorbed his warm weight with a
satisfied little moan. A sweet, drugging lethargy
swept through her as she clung to the hard muscles
of his back.

It seemed so natural and so right to lie with him
this way, as they had lain together that late summer
weekend when they had created their baby. With a
small sigh she opened herself to him, and he entered
with a bold, firm thrust. The thought tumbled dizzily
through her passion-drugged mind that he was part
of her now. An integral part of her, just as their child
was.

He moved sensuously within her, and she was
drawn into a spiraling vortex from which she could
not escape, nor did she want to. Only Adam could
evoke these intense feelings in her, these sensuous,
voluptuous responses. The ecstasy of that weekend

together was recaptured and repeated. An exquisite tension built within her, and she cried Adam's name, shuddering and clinging to him.

"Yes, yes, yes." His voice was husky in her ear. "Just hold onto me and let it happen."

Without warning her body seemed to explode into mind-bending paroxysms of pleasure that sent her spinning into another realm, a wondrous, timeless dimension. When he clutched her convulsively and called out her name, she knew Adam had joined her there.

They were a long time resurfacing. Shay lay silently in Adam's arms, her cheek pressed against his chest, her arm draped loosely across his waist. She couldn't seem to think, and for that she was grateful. A disturbing postmortem on the implication of her response and surrender was inevitable, but at the moment she wanted nothing more than to lie in Adam's arms, satiated and deliciously replete.

Adam petted her with long, languid strokes and she sighed softly. "Sleepy?" he asked at last, brushing her temple with his lips.

She nodded, unable to rouse the energy for a spoken reply.

"You should sleep very well." Adam laughed softly, stroking her eyelids shut with a feather-light caress. "Go to sleep, Shay Kathleen. Sleep in my arms."

Shay couldn't summon the strength to open her eyes again. She felt Adam tuck the covers around them before settling comfortably into the pillows.

The shrill ring of the telephone jarred her awake hours later. A thin shaft of pale December sunlight shone through a gap in the curtains as Shay drowsily fumbled for the phone.

"Hello?" Her voice was thick with sleep.

"Shay? This is Paul."

Shay came instantly awake and sat up with a startled gasp. "Paul! Oh no, it's"—she glanced quickly at the bedside alarm clock, which had not been set the night before—"eight-thirty!"

"And on a Monday morning, too," Paul commiserated cheerfully. "When you didn't arrive for your first-period art class, I thought I'd better call. This is the first day since I came to Carver that you weren't here before me."

"Yes." Shay groaned. She was never late for school and was seldom absent. She'd last missed a day three years ago.

"Did you oversleep?" Paul sounded amused.

Shay stole a glance at Adam, who lay on his back beside her. He was awake, his gray eyes assessing her. She caught the sheet and pulled it to her chin, blushing. "Yes." She choked out the word. "I did. I'll be there right away, Paul."

"No," Adam growled in a low voice, closing his fingers around the soft flesh of her upper arm. "Tell him you won't be in today."

Shay stared at his hand, mesmerized by the sight of it on her pale skin. It was a large hand, the fingers long and lean, the nails squared and immaculate. An experienced hand, one that had caressed and explored every inch of her, learning every intimate, secret place and transporting her out of this world into a mindless ecstasy. The sensual memories rolled over her, and involuntarily her eyes sought Adam's. He met and held her gaze. Desire flickered in the slate-gray depths, and she felt a kindling response to it deep within her.

"Tell him, Shay," he repeated, and she obeyed automatically and without question.

"Paul, I—I won't be in today, after all." It was difficult to breathe, let alone concoct an excuse for her absence. The tightness in her abdomen radiated lower, and she shifted self-consciously. "The reason I overslept is, er, because I'm sick." She watched Adam's lips curve into a slow, sexy smile that made her wriggle again. "Nothing serious. Just a bug, I think."

"Well, you stay in bed and take care of yourself."

Paul's voice was warm with concern. "We want you to get well and come back to school as soon as possible."

Adam shifted his hand to the nape of her neck and began a sensuous massage. Shay's eyes closed involuntarily.

"I thought we'd call in Rachel Jackson to sub," Paul continued. "Not that there could be any adequate substitute for you, Shay."

Adam's fingers blazed an erotic trail along the length of her spine. She shivered.

"Thank you, Paul."

"I mean it, Shay. Would you like me to drop by after school? If there's anything you need or want, I'd be glad to bring it to you."

Adam's lips nuzzled an ultrasensitive spot in the small of her back. Shay swallowed back a moan. "That's kind of you, Paul, but not necessary," she said breathlessly.

"You do sound weak, Shay. I'd better let you get some rest. Call me if you need anything."

Adam removed the receiver from Shay's nerveless fingers and carefully replaced it in its cradle. "You sound weak, Shay," he repeated, a wicked grin lighting his face. "But you aren't going to get much rest in bed, are you?"

He lowered her back onto the mattress.

Eight

"No, Adam, you can't," she breathed, but her protest sounded more like a sigh of pleasure. "I won't let you. . . ." She reeled on the brink of almost unbearable excitement. Her brain clouded, and she stopped in mid-sentence, unable to complete the thought.

"You're so soft here, so moist," Adam soothed huskily. "Like velvet and cream."

She whimpered his name and arched her hips, abandoning all attempts to resist. Her initial reason for doing so now was fuzzzy and remote, completely unrelated to the tempting urgency of the moment. When he came to her, she was transported into that magical world she had entered the night before, a world she wanted to share with Adam again and again.

She was hooked, Shay admitted glumly, standing under the pulsing hot stream of the shower. And Adam knew it. This morning's passionate session had merely confirmed it for them both. When he touched her, she was lost. All the solid reasons why she shouldn't allow it, all the differences between them, faded into oblivion when he took her in his arms.

Shame washed over her as she saw herself in her mind's eye, moving beneath Adam's strong body. She had writhed sensuously, enjoying the feel of his muscled hardness against her complementing softness. He had moved within her, deeply, erotically, and she had loved it and wanted it to go on and on.

Shay choked back a small sob of despair. Permitting herself to give in to her body's craving was a dangerous mistake, one that could only bring her pain. She must not let herself come to need this man, to depend upon him and hope for happiness with him. It would never work, and she would be left the loser, alone and embittered, like her mother before her. And if she were to succumb to an act of sheer idiocy and fall in love with him . . .

Well, she wouldn't, Shay told herself flatly. Sex and love weren't inevitably intertwined. Hadn't Candy told her often enough that sex was the reality and love the illusion? Candy had never been stupid enough to confuse the two. Neither had Case. They had affairs—plenty of sex was involved, but never their emotions. No, they never allowed themselves to become at all emotionally involved. There was no reason why their little sister couldn't follow their lead, Shay vowed. When the time came for Adam to leave her—and she knew it would come—she would simply be losing a sex partner, not the man she loved. And as both Candy and Case were forever affirming, partners in affairs were easily replaced, quite interchangeable.

Shay was drying herself with a lavender bath towel when the doorknob rattled impatiently. "Hey, in there, did you leave me any hot water?" Adam gave a peremptory knock, then rattled the knob again.

Shay quickly wound the towel around her, sarong-style, and opened the door. "The bathroom's yours, Adam."

"You didn't have to lock the door, honey. When you turned down my invitation to shower together, I understood that you preferred your privacy while bathing." Adam stood before her, wearing nothing but a sexy smile.

Shay blushed scarlet and averted her eyes.

"My blushing little bride." Adam grinned, cupping her hips with his big hands to draw her closer. He nuzzled her neck lightly. "Mmm, you smell delicious. Your lilac soap?"

Shay nodded, and felt obliged to add, "If you don't want to use it, I keep some unscented soap in the cabinet under the sink."

"Maybe I'd better use that." Adam gathered her closer. "If I were to go into the office reeking of lilacs, my upstanding, conservative image would be seriously compromised."

"You're going into the office today?" Shay allowed herself to lean into the warmth of his hard, nude body. It was only sex, she reminded herself severely. What had been Candy's pet phrase from the sixties? "If it feels good, do it." She would adopt that philosophy in her sexual relationship with Adam.

"Unfortunately I have a two o'clock conference that I can't miss." Adam stroked her damp hair, which she had piled on top of her head. "But we'll have time to move a few of your things from here to my house."

"My clothes and the kittens," Shay decided. "And my paints." It came as something of a shock to realize that she wanted him to kiss her, and before her brain could process this information she had lifted her face to his. He read the invitation in her eyes. One large hand encircled her nape, and his mouth descended slowly to hers.

The kiss was long and slow and deep. Shay's arms twined around his neck as she pressed closer to him. The towel, forgotten, slipped to the floor.

"Are you sure you won't join me in the shower?" Adam smiled seductively, kneading the rounded firmness of her buttocks. There was no question that he intended to do more than shower, should she agree.

Before she could reply, her stomach rumbled a loud

protest. It was hours past her usual breakfast time. "I'd better eat something." She retrieved the towel and drew it around her. An empty stomach tended to nauseate her.

"I was going to make some coffee, but I couldn't find any," he said, following her through the bedroom.

"I haven't been buying it because I've been avoiding caffeine. I tried the decaffeinated kind, but the smell of it brewing . . ." She made a face.

Adam nodded his understanding. "Have you been sick very often during your pregnancy, Shay?"

"Not really. There were a few things that actually made me gag during the first couple of months, though," she recalled with a grimace as they walked into the kitchen. "The smell of bacon frying or meat cooking, the sight of an egg. Luckily, that's past now." It seemed strange to be sharing these obscure little details of her condition with him, stranger still that he seemed interested. She reached into the small refrigerator and removed a carton of orange juice. "Would you like some juice, Adam?" she offered shyly.

"I'm afraid I'll have to hold out for coffee. We can stop at a fast-food place on the way to Potomac."

"A self-confessed coffee addict." Shay smiled. "You sound just like Paul."

"Who's Paul?"

Shay slipped two slices of whole wheat bread into the toaster. "Paul Deroy, the guidance counselor at school."

"Was he the one who called this morning? A special friend of yours as well?"

"Oh, yes, Paul is a dear friend," Shay said enthusiastically. "I admire him so much. He's marvelous with the kids, completely devoted to them, and they know it and respond accordingly."

Piercing gray eyes narrowed speculatively. "Have you ever dated him, Shay?"

"Yes." She frowned at the memory. "But we stopped dating a year ago."

"Your decision, not his," Adam stated flatly.

"Well, yes." Shay regarded him curiously. "How did you know?"

"Instinct."

"Candy has great faith in lawyerly instincts."

Adam didn't smile. "Does Deroy know about the baby?"

Shay shook her head. "I haven't told anyone at school . . . yet."

"Tell them tomorrow," Adam ordered bluntly. "And make sure your dear friend Deroy knows that you are very much married to me." He whirled away, and a few seconds later she heard the bathroom door slam shut. Seconds later, the water ran hard in the shower.

She fixed herself a bowl of bran cereal and sat down to eat her breakfast, pondering his cryptic commands.

"Well, how do you like it?" Adam asked, turning to Shay as they concluded the tour of his ten-room, Tudor-style house. Spacious, elegantly and perfectly furnished in complementing shades of blue, beige, and rose by one of Washington's leading decorators, the house radiated the upper-class style one would expect a highly successful attorney to have.

"It's beautiful," Shay said politely. Privately she was dismayed. The place had all the warmth and personality of a designer's showroom. It didn't hold a clue to the interests and tastes of its owner. There was not a photograph or personal artifact to be found, only the relentless theme of blue, beige, and rose. Beautifully done but lifeless and anonymous. A house but not a home, she concluded grimly. Even the impressive coffee-table books (with their covers of blue, beige, and rose) positioned just so on the brass-and-glass table in the living room had an untouched quality about them. Shay was sure they had been chosen for their covers.

For some reason the coordinated, impersonal perfection annoyed her. The thought of living in this showplace was distinctly unappealing. "Where can I put my paints and my records?" she asked, glancing dubiously around the oak-paneled den. Adam's extensive record collection lined two shelves of the built-in wall unit, which also housed an intimidatingly expensive stereo system. Even the record jackets seemed to be arranged in complementing shades, Shay noted with astonishment.

"Your records can go right over here." Adam indicated some available space in the unit. He watched her arrange her stack of albums next to his collection of classical composers and Broadway show tunes. "Conway Twitty, Waylon Jennings, Charlie Pride?" His eyes widened with incredulity. "Do you actually listen to this stuff?"

"Yes, I do." Shay was accustomed to defending her tastes in music. Candy had never been able to comprehend her preferences either, and the kids at Carver High were soul devotees. All hooted at Shay's love of anything country. "I suppose you consider yourself superior because you prefer a different type of music?"

"Sweetheart, Bach and Vivaldi and Irving Berlin are certainly superior to Hank Williams and Tammy Wynette." He read the album covers with a condescending amusement that immediately aroused her ire.

"Look, if you feel that my records aren't good enough to mix with yours, I'll just put them somewhere else. Maybe there's a corner in the basement or attic I could have for my own."

"Shay, this whole house is your own now." Adam made no effort to conceal his exasperation. "You're moving in today, remember? This is your home."

Shay thought of her cozy apartment, with its purple furnishings and plants and bright drawings on the walls. "No, Adam, it's your home. I'm just a temporary occupant."

"I don't want you to feel that way, honey." Adam reached for her, but she deftly stepped away.

"How can I not? You won't even let me bring the kittens in from the car."

"I've already explained that Maria doesn't care for animals, Shay. Give me a chance to break it to her first."

"Is that why you keep your poor dog outside in that old doghouse? To placate that cleaning fanatic out there sterilizing the kitchen? Which already looks immaculate, I might add."

"Maria happens to be an excellent housekeeper, Shay. She came to me highly recommended." A spark of anger glimmered in his gray eyes. "I've always been quite satisfied with her work."

"Good." Shay buttoned her coat, which she hadn't bothered to remove since entering the house forty-five minutes before. "I hope the two of you will live happily ever after in this blue-and-beige laboratory." She stalked across the room. "If you enjoy eating off the floor, this is certainly the place for you. A speck of dirt wouldn't dare appear."

"Shay, come back here! Where do you think you're going?"

She slammed the front door behind her, effectively cutting off his objections. Her old blue Buick was parked in front of the house in the wide circular driveway. Adam had not invited her to put it inside the quadruple garage adjoining the house. No doubt the streamlined navy Porsche and the cream-colored Lotus that dwelled within would strenuously object. The Mercedes, which was usually housed there as well, was currently awaiting new tires at the dealership.

The kittens greeted her noisily as she climbed into her car. All three had been enthusiastically exploring their new quarters. Smoky was perched on top of the dashboard, Spats leaped from the front seat to the back in a series of balletlike jumps, and Sinclair was pawing frantically at the windows in a wild bid for freedom.

"We don't belong here, guys," Shay said, watching

Adam stalk grimly toward the car. She had been wrong to assume that she could last even five months in such a sterile environment under the command of that tyrannically tidy housekeeper. She hadn't been able to tolerate it for an hour.

Adam rapped on the car window, and Shay rolled it partway down, keeping her eyes fixed ahead.

"Are you going to sit out here and sulk, Shay?"

"No, I'm going home. It's no use, Adam, I can't stay in—"

"Don't start, Shay," he warned. "You were determined to hate my house. You were stiff as a ramrod from the moment you walked in the front door."

"I don't belong here, Adam."

"Of course you do. You're my wife, Shay."

She sent him a scathing glance. "Temporarily, Adam. Very temporarily."

His lips thinned into a straight, angry line. "I want you to come inside, Shay. Now."

"I—"

"If you don't come willingly, I'll carry you. Come to think of it, it was remiss of me not to have carried you over the threshold the first time we entered the house."

He pulled open the car door and reached for her. Shay scooted nervously across the seat. "No, Adam. I won't let you carry me and I won't come back in, either."

Adam slid behind the wheel and closed the car door. "Unless?"

"What do you mean? Unless what?"

"You tell me. I haven't forgotten that you're Candace Flynn's sister. She never gives unless she gets, and you've absorbed her lessons well. What are your terms, Shay? What do I have to do to get you inside my house?"

Smoky settled himself on Shay's lap, and she stroked his fur absently. "I want to bring the kittens inside."

"I've already agreed to that."

"And I'd like a space of my own, somewhere I can put my paints and easels and—and some of the things from my own living room. I really don't mind using a corner of the basement, Adam. I realize my purple furniture would, uh, clash with the rest of the house."

"Use one of the bedrooms. There are five of them; we can easily convert one into a studio for you. You can bring your furniture and recarpet and rewallpaper, too. In purple, if you wish."

"Do you mean it?" She glanced at him in surprise. The decorator would probably have cardiac arrest at the sight.

"Yes, I mean it." He touched her cheek with the tips of two long fingers. "Now will you come inside, Shay?"

She nodded, bewildered by his extravagant concession. It was because he was so rich, she decided as she followed him back to the house, carrying all three kittens. He probably didn't view redecorating the bedroom as anything more than a trifling annoyance.

The kittens took to their new home with their customary gusto. There was so much to see and do: silk flowers to chew on, vases to knock over, new curtains to climb. Within fifteen minutes of their arrival an irate Maria was upbraiding Adam in a furious torrent of Spanish.

Shay left them and walked out onto the huge patio, just off the formal dining room. Along the tree-lined edge of the property, a few hundred yards from the house, stood a wooden doghouse and a fenced-in run. Bruno, a hefty black Labrador retriever with soulful brown eyes, rested beside the lean-to in front of his house and watched her approach.

"It's cold out here," she said to the dog as she let herself into the small compound. Bruno stood up, wagging his tail a bit uncertainly.

"Why don't you come inside and meet your new roommates, Bruno? I hope you won't mind that they're cats." She patted the huge black head, and the dog gave her a warm look of gratitude. Or so it seemed to Shay. She melted.

"It's not fair for you to be out in the cold all the time while Maria sanitizes an already spotless house." She kept up a steady stream of conversation as the dog trotted along beside her. When they reached the door, Bruno hesitated and began to whine.

"Come on, Bruno," she coaxed. "We're both moving in today." Bruno accepted the invitation and entered, his head held high in a regal display of canine pride.

Five minutes later Maria announced she was quitting.

Shay absented herself from the housekeeper's leave-taking to watch Bruno's amazed reaction to the three kittens' rather tentative overtures of friendship. When Adam joined them later in the den, he found Bruno dozing at Shay's feet while the kittens pranced over and about the furniture, Bruno, and Shay. A soulful country duet wailed from the stereo speakers.

"Is Maria gone?" Shay asked. It was difficult to contain her relief. She was convinced the housekeeper had hated her on sight. She had certainly hated the animals!

"I gave her a month's severance pay and drove her to the bus stop." Adam shook his head. "She'll be working for the Leightons by tomorrow morning. You drove her away, Shay. Letting Bruno inside was the last straw, as you well know."

"It seemed so unfair, letting the cats inside and keeping poor Bruno out."

"Poor Bruno! He's a tough hunting dog, an outdoor dog. He thoroughly enjoyed his life."

She leaned down to stroke the sleek black fur. "Well, now he'll like it even better, won't you, Bruno, old boy?"

"I won't let you turn him into a pampered lapdog, sweetheart. Isn't it enough that you've gotten rid of my housekeeper and intend to turn one of my bedrooms purple?" Adam stared at her as she patted the dog and wondered why he wasn't furious with her. In the course of two days she had managed to turn his carefully organized life upside down. And yet . . .

The plaintive voice of Tammy Wynette lamenting D-I-V-O-R-C-E filled the room and Adam frowned. With an abrupt exclamation, he strode across the room to the turntable. Spats leaped at his leg and clung to his trousers with sharp little claws. Adam shook him off with a muttered oath. "I've heard enough of this caterwauling, Shay. If you want to listen to music, I'll put on Rachmaninoff."

Shay stood up and walked to the door. "Never mind, Adam. I think I'll unpack now."

"You'd rather do that than listen to music that will enhance you, enrich your life . . ."

"I take vitamins for that," she said cheekily.

Adam scowled, and suddenly Shay smiled. "I'm teasing you, Adam. I'm not quite the lowbrow you think I am."

A reluctant grin teased the corners of Adam's mouth. There was something about her smile he found fascinating, irresistible, and he felt his irritation begin to fade. "Your suitcases are in the master bedroom," he said. "Use the closet on the left."

The immense, walk-in closet was nearly the size of Shay's bedroom in her apartment. Her rather limited wardrobe filled less than one-sixth of it, and her four pairs of shoes looked lost on the shoe rack, designed to hold fifty pairs.

Adam viewed the spectacle with a frown. "You're going shopping, Shay. This afternoon."

Well, she did need some maternity clothes, Shay conceded silently. And since she'd taken the day off school, she might as well use the time to shop for them.

"My meeting shouldn't last longer than an hour," Adam continued. "Then we'll go shopping."

"We?" Shay echoed. "Are you coming with me?"

"Definitely. I want to be certain that you buy—"

"What you consider suitable, proper clothes," Shay

inserted caustically. "I mustn't be more of an embarrassment to you than I am already."

A dark flush stained his neck and crept upward to his face. "Don't put words in my mouth!"

"Well, it's true, isn't it? You find my clothes appalling." She eyed him curiously. "I forgot to ask if you'd notified your family of the calamity."

"The calamity being our wedding?" Adam didn't smile. "Yes, I called them this morning while you were in the shower."

"And were they properly appalled? Unduly horrified?"

"Shay, your flippancy tends to become a bit wearing at times."

"Ha! They were!"

Adam grimaced. "My parents were a bit, er, disconcerted by the news. After all, they had never heard me mention you, and to announce suddenly that we're married . . ."

"Did you tell them about the baby, Adam?"

"I had to tell them," Adam replied, his tone defensive. "They're capable of counting to nine, Shay. And the baby is going to be born on number five." There was a moment's silence. "They want to meet you, of course. I suggested that they come to visit us next weekend."

"Next weekend?" Shay was unable to suppress a groan of dismay. She was scarcely adjusted to Adam, and the prospect of meeting his parents was terrifying. She was certain they would hate her.

"My sister and brother-in-law will also be coming i· from New York that weekend. I thought we migh have a little party on Saturday night while they're all here, to introduce you to some of my friends as well."

"That's the worst idea I've ever heard!" Shay burst out. A party with herself as the evening's entertainment, the object of speculation and criticism and condescension? It was a social nightmare come true. "Please no, Adam. That's just a few days before Christmas. And I know it'll be a disaster."

"Of course it won't. It'll be fun, Shay. Just the family and a few good friends. We'll make it a Christmas party, and I know you'll enjoy yourself."

Shay stared at him in disbelief. Fun? Was he serious? She supposed he was. Adam Wickwire would have been blessed with social poise and confidence at birth. He could never comprehend the insecurities of a Shay Flynn.

"I have some pride, too, Adam. The Wickwires don't hold a monopoly on it, you know." Her lips twisted into a tight little smile. "Your family and friends will see me as a scheming gold-digger who trapped poor, noble you into marriage. I can't handle a whole evening of that!"

"Shay, we both know that you aren't a gold-digger and that our marriage was at my insistence. You're making far too much of this party, sweetheart. I refuse to argue the issue any further. We'll hire a caterer. And I'll call the agency tomorrow about a replacement for Maria."

Glumly Shay conceded defeat—to a point. "I'm going to invite Case and Candy, no matter what you say."

"Fine. I'll invite them myself. I want your family to meet mine. I'm not the villain you persist in making me, Shay."

Shay turned away, unaware of his tentatively outstretched hand. No, Adam wasn't a villain. He was a man who accepted responsibility, a man who followed the dictates of his conscience even when it was diametrically opposed to his wishes. Why else would he have insisted on marrying the woman who had tricked him into impregnating her? Case, the man she admired most in the world, would have done no such thing. He would have hired Candy to scare the woman off!

Nine

Although Adam insisted that she accompany him to his office later that afternoon, she could tell that he wasn't pleased with her outfit. In a full-cut denim jumper, an orchid jersey, and matching tights, with her hair in two thick French braids, Shay knew that she looked just fine for a day at Carver High—but she hardly fit the part of the wife of an established Washington attorney.

"It's one of my best outfits," she muttered as they drove into the city. "If you'd rather, I'll wait in the car for you."

"Paranoia, another one of your endearing personality traits." Adam heaved an exasperated sigh. "Shay, did I say one critical word about your clothes? About your appearance? Did I give even the slightest hint that I am less than pleased about taking you with me to the office?"

"No, but—"

"No buts. You aren't going to wait in the car for me. You're coming with me to meet everyone."

And meet everyone she did. From the moment Adam ushered her inside a plush office building in a

tree-lined section of northwest Washington, Shay
was introduced to a seemingly endless stream of sec-
retaries, paralegals, junior partners, and associates.
Paulette Wilder greeted her effusively, like a longtime
friend.

"I knew Shay before she was the boss's wife," the
younger woman explained airily to the others.

Shay caught Adam's eye and grinned. Her! The
boss's wife!

The two senior partners, John W. Sinclair and
William K. Prescott, were presented to her in their
own enormous, book-lined private offices.

"Well, you certainly surprised us, Tripp." Adam's
uncle, Bill Prescott, stared unabashedly at Shay. Surprise was obviously a euphemism for his true senti-
ments: shock, disappointment, disbelief. Or so it
seemed to Shay.

"I've been a bachelor long enough, Bill," Adam
replied heartily. "I decided it was time to settle down
and sample the pleasures of wedded bliss."

Trying to hide her nervousness, Shay turned her
attention to the printed genealogy hanging on the
wall. The chart was quite complete, with all branches
of the family tree duly recorded. She studied all the
names, lingering on the three Adam Prescott Wickwires. Although she didn't know the names of all her
great-grandparents, the Prescott-Wickwires traced
their bloodlines back hundreds of years. And her
baby would be part of it all, she thought with wonder.

"I'm inviting all the attorneys in the firm to a party
next Saturday, Bill. I hope that you and Aunt Frances
will come."

Adam's words sent Shay spinning out of her reverie. A small party, he had said. With the family and a
few friends. She must have met at least fifty lawyers
associated with this firm today! Shay emitted a
horrified gasp.

Bill Prescott seemed equally appalled. "All the attorneys, Tripp? That would include"—he cleared his

throat and glanced uneasily at Shay—"er—Bunny Warrington."

"Yes," Adam replied coolly. "She isn't in her office now, but I plan to invite her as soon as I see her."

Shay stared at him, aghast. Surely Adam didn't intend to invite his girlfriend to the party . . . the party at which he introduced his wife!

"Tripp, I'm not trying to cause trouble, but I think you should know that Bunny is quite upset." The older man appeared clearly uncomfortable with the topic. He lowered his voice. "I mentioned your marriage this morning and it seemed to come as a complete surprise to her. Although I'm aware that there was no definite commitment between you two, I'm afraid Bunny—"

"You're correct, Bill. There was no definite commitment, on either of our parts," Adam interrupted tautly.

"Bunny is in court today, although I wish she weren't." Bill Prescott sighed. "I tried to talk her into seeking a delay, but she wouldn't hear of it. The Morrison divorce case. Unfortunately, Mrs. Morrison is being represented by none other than Candace Flynn."

"Bunny is a damn good lawyer." Adam sounded annoyed. "She just might hold her own against Candace Flynn."

"Bunny docs fine with estates, but she's no match for a bomber like Flynn in a contested divorce, and we both know it, Tripp. Candace Flynn is the most lethal divorce lawyer in town, and she trounced Bunny two other times in court. I didn't want Bunny to handle Jock Morrison's divorce, but she insisted. She has some sort of vendetta going against Flynn and wants to win this one."

Great, Shay thought, groaning silently. Adam's former girlfriend locked in a courtroom feud with Candy. Yet another complication in her hopelessly complex relationship with Adam.

"It might interest you to know that Candace Flynn

is Shay's older sister." Adam imparted that information a bit reluctantly.

Bill Prescott's gray eyes, so like his nephew's, glimmered with sudden admiration. "Well." He looked at Shay as if seeing her for the first time. "Candace Flynn's sister, eh? Why didn't you say so in the first place, Adam?"

"I didn't realize you were such a fan of Ms. Flynn's, Bill."

"I'm dazzled by her string of six- and seven-figure divorce settlements." The older man chuckled. "You'd better treat this little girl very well, Tripp," he added with increasing jocularity. "You can't afford to tangle with Candy Flynn over her sister!"

Shay smiled wanly. If mentioning her sister's prowess had caused a definite thaw in Bill Prescott's attitude, it had also produced a definite freeze in Adam's. He hustled her out of his uncle's office without another word.

"Wait here in the reception area until I've finished with my client," he ordered, and Shay waited, sobered by his icy mien.

She guessed he was angered by his uncle's reminder of Candy's successes over Bunny Warrington. Did that mean he felt protective of his colleague—who had been much more than a colleague? Perhaps he cared more for this Bunny Warrington than he wanted to admit. The thought depressed Shay more than *she* wanted to admit. Bad enough to be married, but to have your husband longing for another woman . . . She swallowed a rising lump in her throat. It was beginning already, the misery that constituted marriage.

"Ready to go, honey?" Adam joined her an hour later, all smiles. He helped her on with her coat, his fingers pausing to caress her nape lightly. "I hope you weren't too bored waiting for me, sweetheart. I didn't expect to take this long."

Shay regarded him with the suspicion one usually reserves for an unfamiliar species. She had braced herself for the coldness he had displayed earlier, had even planned her own display of cool indifference. His unexpected friendliness disarmed her. How was she supposed to respond to this display of warmth?

"First we're going to buy you some rings." Adam tucked her hand into the crook of his elbow as he guided her out of the building. There had been no time to buy a ring before the hasty ceremony, so they had made use of Adam's college ring, which Shay had returned to him immediately after the judge pronounced them man and wife.

"A wedding band, of course, and an engagement ring as well." He gave her a heart-stopping smile that seemed to warm her like a snifter of potent brandy. "Although our overnight engagement is probably one of the shortest on record."

There wasn't a price tag to be seen in the exclusive jewelry store where Adam took her. Clearly the policy here was: "If you have to ask, you can't afford it." Adam didn't ask. He simply chose a sparkling sapphire-and-diamond ring and a thick gold band, and when she approved, slipped them on her finger.

The sight of the rings on her finger underscored the aura of unreality that marked the rest of the day. Adam whisked her from shop to shop, outfitting her from head to foot, inside and out, helping her to choose a complete maternity wardrobe with the expertise and patience of a veteran shopper. He carried the growing stack of packages without complaint, ordering later purchases to be sent to the house. Shay was overwhelmed by his generosity. She felt like a princess; no one had ever indulged her so.

Since they were both starving by seven o'clock, they decided to eat at a Chinese restaurant in town before heading back to Adam's house in Potomac.

"I made arrangements with a moving company to move your furniture from your apartment to the house. The stuff should arrive by the end of the week," Adam told her over an appetizer of shrimp-

and-spinach egg rolls. "You can begin fixing up your studio next week."

The offer, coming after his largesse of the afternoon, took her breath away. "I don't know how to thank you, Adam." She stared at him, bemused. He didn't have to do these things for her, a tiny voice inside her head prompted. He had married her out of a sense of obligation, but that obligation didn't include showering her with gifts, allowing her to change his home, indulging her outrageously.

"I can think of a way." Adam smiled wickedly. "Can't you, sweetheart?"

Color rose in her cheeks as a hot warmth flooded her. Yesterday she would have been thrown into a panic by his blatant suggestion; today she felt a tingling sexual excitement. Adam stretched his long legs under the table, sliding one possessively between her ankles . . . reminding her of that first night, her seduction of him.

Although they conversed pleasantly on neutral topics throughout dinner and during the drive home, a powerful sexual tension continued to build, entangling them both in its tentacles.

"Let's leave the packages in the car," Adam said huskily as he pulled the Porsche into the garage and braked to a stop. "I'll bring them in later."

Shay nodded her agreement, willing herself to breathe normally. All evening the hot, tight feeling in her loins had been growing, and her entire body was aching for his touch. When Adam opened the car door and extended his hand to help her out, she accidentally—or was it deliberately? Shay couldn't be certain—brushed her breasts against his arm. Adam responded at once by pulling her against him. She sighed and snuggled nearer as his mouth closed hungrily over hers. The kiss was urgent and brief. Adam scooped her up and carried her inside without another word.

The telephone began to ring the moment Adam reached the stairs. Shay buried her face in the curve of his shoulder and stifled a disappointed groan. She wanted him so badly; she felt like yanking the intrusive telephone from its jack. The force of her desire astonished her and worried her. She had been married for all of two days and already craved her husband's loving like a junkie craving a fix. How much longer until she was hopelessly, pathetically addicted?

"As much as I'd like to ignore it, I suppose I ought to answer the phone," Adam said heavily, reluctantly setting her to her feet. "Why don't you go upstairs and undress and wait for me in bed, darling?"

Shay chose to feed the animals instead. The image of herself lying naked in bed, waiting for Adam to come to her, was too unsettling to pursue. Bruno and the kittens wolfed down their meals, liberally sampling each other's food, and when they were finished Adam had yet to reappear. Shay lifted the receiver of the kitchen phone and held it tentatively to her ear. She was surprised to find the line free. Did Adam have two separate lines, as did Candy, or was he finished with his caller? She decided to find out.

The door to his study was tightly closed, but Shay could hear his muffled tones as she stood in the blue carpeted hallway. Two lines, then. Returning to the kitchen, she paced restlessly for a few minutes before deciding to make use of the phone herself.

"Candy?"

"Shay! Oh, honey, I'm so glad you called. I've been trying to reach you for two days. Where have you been?"

"Getting married. I partially moved into Adam's place today." Shay's eyes drifted to the set of rings on her third finger, left hand.

"Oh." There was a long pause. "Shay, I don't know what to say." Neither did Shay.

"I'm sorry that idiot David blurted out the story the way he did," Candy said at last. "It was a particularly unpleasant way for Adam to, er, learn he was to be a father."

"Tell me about it," Shay muttered.

"Honey, I know how you feel about marriage—God knows I feel the same—but in this case I can't help but feel it's for the best," Candy said bracingly. "Having an illegitimate child simply isn't practical, nor is it fair to the child. And it won't be for long, Shay. You know I'll bail you out of this mess with a very tidy settlement as soon as the baby is born."

"Yes, I know, Candy." Shay's heart turned to lead in her chest. She seemed to have no say in the matter. Adam and Candy had decided what was to be done. He had engineered the marriage; Candy would handle the divorce. Shay felt like a Ping-Pong ball volleyed between the two. How had she managed to lose control of her own life? She dispiritedly said good-bye to her sister.

"Mapping out your strategy already?"

Shay jumped at the sound of Adam's voice. He stood in the doorway of the kitchen, his face a mask of cold contempt. "What do you mean?"

"I needed to make a call on the other line. When I picked up the phone to dial, I overheard you and your sister discussing her plans for a tidy settlement when she bails you out of this mess. End quote."

Shay's mouth went dry. "Adam, I'm—"

"It's not going to work, Shay." Adam advanced toward her, his gray eyes menacing. "Your sister isn't going to fleece me the way she did Jock Morrison." He stood directly in front of her, towering above her. "Incidentally, that was Morrison on the phone. He wanted to tell me that he's withdrawing his business from Wickwire, Prescott & Sinclair. He's so furious with Bunny Warrington's representation of him in his divorce that he intends to sever his association with the firm completely."

"That's unfair of him. He should have never expected a corporate firm like yours to handle his divorce. It's not your specialty," Shay hastened to point out. "He could have hired Candy himself, or someone like her. Candy says—"

"Candy says," Adam mimicked with a sneer. "Exactly how tidy a settlement does she intend to grab when she 'bails you out of this mess'?"

A wave of protective sympathy washed over Shay. Poor Adam. How he would hate to be the object of one of Candy's much-heralded triumphs. He didn't deserve such humiliation.

She tried to reassure him. "I won't let Candy press for one of her gigantic settlements, I promise, Adam." She raised earnest blue eyes to him. "You can decide what's a fair amount of child support and that's all I'll accept. Not a cent more."

Adam muttered an oath and stalked furiously from the kitchen.

It was a bleak ending to an emotionally charged day, and Shay approached the master bedroom with trepidation. The warm desire she had felt earlier had died. Now she was exhausted and sought only the oblivion of sleep. Adam was already in the king-sized bed when she entered the bedroom. He didn't stir or speak, although she knew he couldn't be asleep. She wondered if she was still supposed to share this room, this bed. Her parents hadn't even been able to share the same roof after one of their numerous quarrels. One of them inevitably stormed out of the house to spend the night, or the next few days, elsewhere.

She slipped quietly into the large, luxurious bathroom, with its blue-, beige-, and rose-colored tiles. After completing her nightly ablutions and changing into her purple flannel nightgown, she crept through the darkened bedroom. She had decided it would be prudent to use one of the spare bedrooms tonight.

The bedside lamp flicked on as she reached the door. "Where are you going?" Adam asked gruffly, positioning himself on one elbow. The goose-down comforter and blue-and-beige-striped sheet were at waist level, exposing his bare chest. The elegant brass bed frame behind him gleamed in the lamplight.

"I—I thought I'd better use one of the other rooms,"

Shay stammered. Her eyes were riveted to his muscular shoulders, the thick mat of wiry dark hair on his chest.

"This is our bedroom, Shay. You'll sleep here."

She nodded, chewing her lips nervously. Adam watched her walk around to the unoccupied side of the big bed. "You're wearing your old nightgown," he remarked as she slipped beneath the covers. "What about the new ones we bought today?"

He had insisted that she buy seven new gowns, silky, feminine creations in different pastel shades. "They're still in the car," Shay whispered. Sudden tears stung her eyes. They had had such fun shopping together this afternoon, and the underlying thread of passion throughout the evening had promised so much. "We were going to bring the packages in—later," she added, trying to choke back a sob.

"Shay?" Adam leaned over her, trailing a finger along her wet cheek. "You're crying."

She was as surprised as he by the discovery. Yes, she was crying. Tears streamed down her face, and her shoulders shook with suppressed sobs.

"Don't cry." Adam touched her arm lightly, tentatively, his voice aloof, yet sounding very uncertain.

Shay rolled onto her side and buried her face in the pillow, unable to stop the tears.

"Shay, please, baby, stop crying." Adam abandoned his restraint and pulled her into his arms. "You'll make yourself sick if you keep on this way."

Shay lay rigid and tense in his embrace, and he began to knead the taut muscles of her neck and shoulders.

"Darling, please don't cry," he soothed softly, comforting her with his words and the magic warmth of his hands.

Slowly Shay began to relax. "I didn't want today to end the way it did, Adam." She raised tear-wet eyes to his.

"Neither did I," he murmured, his lips moving gently over her cheeks, her jawline, the curve of her chin. His hands slowly lifted the hem of her night-gown. "I wanted it to end like this."

Shay sighed softly as he removed the gown and eased her back onto the mattress. Her arms encircled his neck, and she drew him down on top of her, smoothing her hands over the hard muscles of his back. She felt weak with relief. Adam didn't hate her; he hadn't ordered her out of his bed or his room or his life. He still wanted her.

His lips sweetly tasted her, and she surged against him, crying his name softly. His hands moved possessively over her abdomen, where their child rested, deep within.

"You're mine, Shay," he whispered fiercely, sliding his hand lower, lower, to close over the heart of her feminine warmth. "You're my wife and you're carrying my child. You belong to me completely."

"Oh, yes, Adam," she breathed as she arched against him. She longed to assert the corollary: that he was hers, her husband and the father of her child. That he belonged to her exclusively and completely. But she didn't dare. Possessive statements on her part might annoy him or make him feel guilty.

And hadn't *Cosmopolitan* sternly advised against laying a guilt trip on a man? It was one of the "Five Quickest Ways to Lose Him." Shay couldn't remember what the other four were, but she was sure that getting pregnant against his wishes ranked right up there, and she had already done that.

"Darling, I can't wait any longer," Adam breathed, moving between her legs. Shay accommodated him willingly. The words she wanted to say might never be said, but she could show him with her body instead. And did.

"Shay, you were fantastic," Adam said with a sigh much later, holding her close in the aftermath of their rapturous whirl into the heights of ecstasy. "You are the most passionate, the most giving, the most abandoned—"

"Adam!" Shay pressed her fingers over his lips in an embarrassed attempt to hush him.

He kissed her fingertips, chuckling. "Did I forget to mention shy?" His mouth took hers in a long, lingering kiss. "It was so good tonight, sweetheart. So very good."

"Yes," she whispered, clinging to him. "So very good."

Adam was still sleeping heavily when Shay reluctantly rolled out of bed at six o'clock the next morning. It was dark outside, and the overnight chill of the house made her shiver. After a quick hot shower she dressed warmly in a pair of new dark green wool slacks, an oversized mauve sweater with a white turtleneck underneath, and her favorite ballet-style shoes. She decided to leave the jeweled engagement ring on the dresser, but the gold wedding band remained firmly affixed to her finger. She wondered if her students would notice. Paul Deroy undoubtedly would.

Bruno and the kittens ate a big breakfast and begged for half of hers. They were all chipper and energetic and would have loved for her to play with them. Shay marveled at their early-morning enthusiasm. She certainly didn't share it.

Having to get up an hour earlier than usual because of the longer commute was particularly horrid on a cold, dark December morning. A few snow flurries swirled around her as she walked to the Buick, parked by the side of the house. It was harder to start in the cold, and a full ten minutes had elapsed before she pulled out of the long, circular driveway.

"I have an announcement to make," she told her first-period art class. "I'm married." She held up her hand, displaying the new wedding ring.

"What's your new name, Miss Flynn?" one of the girls demanded.

"Mrs. Wickwire." It was the first time she had used

the name, and a peculiar little thrill ran through her. Shay Kathleen Wickwire.

By the end of the day, her last-period art class made it unanimous. All of the students hated her new name. None of them could get it right, and after hearing variations of Wirewick, Warwick, and Wicker, Shay gave up and suggested that they stick to Miss Flynn. A prescient suggestion? she wondered.

By dismissal time, the flurries had turned to large flakes, but since a major snowstorm was not predicted for the area, Shay decided to hold the Art Club meeting as scheduled.

"So what's your old man like, Miss Flynn?" Jerad asked, staring curiously at the thick gold band on her finger.

"He's her new man," Anthony corrected. "Her new main man."

The students laughed.

"Are we going to meet him?" Tiana asked excitedly. "Is he going to come caroling with us?"

"I don't know, Tiana." Shay tried and failed to picture Adam with this group. "He's very busy. But I'll, um, ask him."

"Is he a good-lookin' dude?" Darlene asked, giggling.

Shay grinned. "A very good-lookin' dude."

There was a good deal of laughter then, and it was some time before the students began to settle down. Soon, though, they all became involved with their holiday collages. When Paul Deroy entered the art room late that afternoon, he had his usual treats for the students, but Shay noticed the strain in his smile.

"I heard the news from everyone," Paul said immediately when he joined her after distributing pretzels and making his usual jokes with the kids. "About you and your husband."

Shay nodded slowly. The fictitious husband she had invented years ago had little in common with the flesh-and-blood one she had so recently acquired. "I came to your office to tell you this morning," she said, "but you were out. I'm sorry you heard it through the grapevine, Paul."

He shrugged. "It wasn't totally unexpected. You've been intimating for some time that you might go back to him. . . ." His voice trailed off. "Shay, would you mind if I asked you a personal question?" She nodded assent. "Are you pregnant? Is that the real reason for this sudden reconciliation?"

Shay shifted uncomfortably. She didn't like lying to Paul. "I'll be applying for maternity leave soon." That much, at least was true. "I'd like to be able to work into May, since the baby isn't due until the end of the month."

There was a long silence. Both watched the students' inexhaustible horseplay without really seeing it. A muscle twitched convulsively in Paul's jaw, but when he spoke, his voice was calm and even. "I just want you to know that I'll always be your friend, Shay. Your baby's, too."

"I'm glad, Paul," she said softly.

"Hey, it's really coming down hard out there!" Jerad yelled, pointing to the window in delight. The sky was already dark and thick snowflakes were falling heavily. "Think they'll call off school tomorrow?"

"It doesn't look like the light nonstorm predicted by the National Weather Service," Shay remarked.

"I called weather after school," Chandra said. "They're predicting we're in for a major snowstorm, with six to eight inches of snow."

"Chandra, I wish you'd mentioned that before now." Shay sighed. Six to eight inches of snow? And she had to drive all the way back to Potomac.

"I guess I forgot," Chandra shrugged.

"Uh-oh, I forgot something, too." Paul slapped his forehead. "Shay, your husband's secretary called the school office about an hour ago." Paul stared out the window at the steadily worsening storm. "She relayed a message from your husband. He wants you to stay in your apartment here in the city tonight and not risk traveling out to Potomac."

"I'm not afraid of a little snow," Shay scoffed. Only moments ago she had viewed the drive out to Potomac with trepidation, but now, faced with the alternative, she was suddenly fearless.

The thought of her empty apartment was singularly unappealing. She wanted to see Adam tonight, she admitted to herself with a dreamy smile. She wanted to have dinner with him and spend the evening with him, to lie in his arms and make love in the big bed.

"The roads will be in miserable shape, Shay," Paul said with a frown. "With no advance warning, there's been no chance for the road crews to clear them."

"We'd better send the kids home now," Shay said, dismissing Paul's words of caution. She had snow tires, and the old Buick was a heavy car. She wanted to go home tonight, and she would. Home to Adam.

Ten

Paul had been absolutely right about the condition of the roads, Shay conceded grimly as she guided the Buick over a particularly treacherous stretch of the Beltway. A number of cars had been abandoned along the side of the road, the drivers having given up in their attempts to navigate through the blizzard. One car ahead of her had careened wildly from side to side, and Shay had narrowly avoided hitting it. She was grateful she had learned to drive in Michigan and had a great deal of experience driving in snow. Some of these hapless Washingtonians were clearly terrified novices.

There were no signs of any road crews with snow-removal equipment, and the radio continually blared out dangerous-driving warnings. And the driving was indeed dangerous. Visibility was severely limited by the thick, swirling flakes of snow, and the car skidded precariously if Shay attempted to go over ten miles an hour.

It took her over four hours to complete the drive that had taken forty-five minutes that morning. The lights of Adam's house beckoned invitingly as Shay steered the Buick into the snow-covered driveway. Her heart began to pound with excited anticipation as she staggered through the wind and snow to the front door. The tension and fatigue brought on by the hazardous drive had already begun to lessen. She rang the doorbell, making a mental note to ask Adam for a key. He was going to be so surprised to see her. . . .

Adam gaped at her as if she were an apparition. "Shay!" Never had she seen him so stunned.

"May I come in?" She smiled, brushing the snow-flakes from her dark lashes.

"But what are you doing here?" Adam caught her arms and pulled her inside, then slammed the door shut. "Did you actually drive the whole way out here in this mess?"

She nodded, her face wreathed in smiles. How handsome he looked in his tan cords and cream-colored fisherman's sweater. She wanted to hurl herself recklessly into his arms.

"Didn't you get my message?" he asked, still obviously shocked. "I told Peggy to call the school and tell you—"

"I know," she interrupted, gazing at him with love-softened eyes. "But I wanted to—"

"Adam, who on earth is at the door? Some stranded motorist?"

Shay's mouth hung open. The voice was a throaty, feminine one. Seconds later a well-dressed blue-eyed blonde joined them in the hallway. "Well." The blonde glanced at Shay's snow-covered form. "And who is this?" Her amusement smacked of condescension, and Shay scowled.

"Shay, this is Bunny Warrington," Adam said quickly. His customary aplomb was noticeably absent. "Bunny, I'd like you to meet my wife, Shay."

Shay stood paralyzed as a spasm of pain struck with the force of a lightning bolt. The pieces clicked instantly into place, just as her headache of the past four hours returned in full force. Bunny Warrington!

She understood now. Adam's message about her staying in town had nothing to do with his concern for her safety. He'd used the weather as an excuse to get rid of her so that he could entertain his girlfriend! Obviously he had a great deal of explaining to do to one Bunny Warrington! Shay cursed herself for blundering into this scene. And she cursed Adam.

"Adam told me that you were staying in town tonight," Bunny said. She seemed to be the only one capable of speech. "Whatever made you venture the whole way out here?"

Shay stared at her. The woman was beautiful, with a polished, sophisticated manner that Shay knew she could never achieve. A wild, primitive fury suddenly raged within her, supplanting the initial staggering pain. She felt an overwhelming desire to claw Bunny Warrington's face of porcelain perfection to shreds and then start in on Adam.

How dare he? She began to tremble violently as a burst of adrenaline surged through her system. She had battled the elements for over four hours to come home to him, only to find him cozily ensconced with an old flame.

"Shay, let me take off that wet coat of yours. You're shivering," Adam began to unbutton her coat with unsteady fingers. He was visibly nervous, Shay noted with malicious satisfaction. Did he think that she would disgrace herself—and him—by creating some terrible scene in front of the lovely Bunny? The idea *was* a tempting one.

But this was her moment of truth. She could prove to herself right now that she had not inherited the uncontrollable, raging tempers that had ruled her parents and ruined their lives. The scene was actually a familiar one to her. How many times as a child had she cowered behind a piece of furniture while her parents battled over her father's latest fling? Screams and curses and threats had been flung from both sides, slaps and punches, too. Any object at hand was a convenient missile to be hurled. It took great willpower not to slug Adam as he solicitously pulled off her coat and gloves, but Shay persevered. She could understand her parents' furies but she need not imitate their behavior. She stepped away from him, inordinately proud of herself. She had done it! She had broken the destructive cycle of family violence. Her own child would never have to endure the terror of an adult's ungovernable emotions.

"Honey, you took a terrible risk, driving in this storm." Adam knelt before her and removed one of her soaked shoes. "The roads are dangerous; you might have had a terrible accident."

Had Shay been her mother, she would have kicked him in the teeth. Instead she endured his ministrations, stepping gracefully out of her other shoe. "I wanted to get back to make sure the kittens were fed." The lie came out easily. She would never admit the silly truth to Adam, that she had been rushing home to him. She might be a fool, but she wasn't a complete idiot.

"Where are the kittens?" she added. They usually appeared at the sound of her voice, but there wasn't a trace of them or Bruno.

"Oh, those awful cats!" Bunny shuddered. "Adam put them outside."

Shay felt her heart stop, then start again with a violent surge. "What?"

"Not outside," Adam corrected quickly. "I put them in the garage. Bunny's afraid of cats, and they wouldn't leave her alone, so—"

"You put my kittens out in the middle of a blizzard?" It was difficult to maintain her rigid control. The spirit of her mother was urging her toward the tall brass candlestick that stood in the corner.

"Shay, the garage is heated, for heaven's sake. The cats are fine." Adam followed her through the hallway, through the kitchen, to the door that connected with the huge garage.

The door was locked. "Give me the keys." Shay's tone was imperious.

Adam unlocked the door in record speed, and she flung it open to find the three kittens huddled together on the small step in front of the door.

She fought back the horrible urge to burst into tears. It didn't matter that the garage was warm, that the kittens were in no danger from the raging storm. Their plight forcefully emphasized her own; on the outside looking in, unwelcome and supplanted in Adam's house. And in his life?

She stooped to pick up Sinclair, while Smoky and Spats raced inside, meowing gleefully.

"You see, they were perfectly all right," Bunny observed sullenly. She had followed Shay and Adam into the kitchen.

"Where's Bruno?" Shay asked coldly, giving the other woman her best imitation-Candy glare. "Are you afraid of dogs, too?"

"He was drooling all over me," Bunny complained. "Adam put him back in his doghouse—where he belongs," she added spitefully.

"I'd like to stuff you in a rabbit hutch, where you belong," Shay muttered under her breath. She set the kitten down and headed for the double glass doors that opened onto the stone patio.

"Shay, the doghouse is well insulated. The dog has spent every winter out there with no ill effects." Adam hurried along beside her, then gasped in horror as she unbolted the doors and stepped outside. "Shay, come back here. You don't have a coat on. Dammit, Shay, you're not even wearing shoes!"

"My, how very impulsive she is!" Bunny sounded pleased.

Shay's fury rendered her impervious to the cold. She wouldn't have been surprised to find the snow melting beneath her stockinged feet, so intense was the heat of her anger. Bruno emerged from the doghouse as she let herself inside the compound. His tail began to wag at the sight of her.

"Shay!" Both she and Bruno turned to see Adam loping toward them. He, too, was coatless, and Shay permitted herself a satisfied sneer at the sight. His little trek through the snow spelled doom for his elegant two-hundred-dollar loafers.

"Shay, I can guess how this must look to you, but let me explain." She ignored him as they trudged back to the house, Bruno leading the way. "Honey, listen to me. Bunny stopped by after work to apologize for her appalling performance in the Morrison divorce case. She knows that Jock dropped us because of her and he was an important client . . ."

Shay said nothing. There was one thing she had learned about lawyers. In a tight corner no one could be faster with his tongue. Candy could virtually talk her way out of anything. Adam, too.

"Shay, Bunny was terribly upset. You see, my uncle talked with her this afternoon and told her that she'd blown any chance of ever making partner in the firm. He and Jack Sinclair are livid about the Morrison case. What they effectively told her, Shay, is that her career with the firm is over, that she'll never advance above junior associate. It mean she'll have to move on or stagnate."

"So she came to cry on your shoulder, knowing that she'd find a sympathetic ear," Shay said calmly. "Did you assure her that you would overrule your mean old uncle?"

"I can't do that, Shay, and Bunny knows it. Since Maria's gone, she offered to cook dinner for me. I'm not much of a cook, and—"

"Oh, that's a nice touch, Adam." Shay flashed a sardonic smile. "The helpless-male-in-the-kitchen bit. Although the story about poor Bunny's career in ruins wasn't bad either. You truly are a credit to your profession."

They entered the house together, and when Shay would have continued out of the dining room, Adam caught her arm. "Shay, do you think I'm lying? Honey, every word I've spoken is true."

"If you don't take your hands off me, I won't be responsible for my actions," Shay gritted through clenched teeth. "I don't care to hear any more of your phony explanations." She couldn't bear to be duped by his lies. He had a nerve even to try!

Wrenching away from him, she stalked upstairs. Reaction was beginning to set in from the cold and from the strain of holding her terrible anger in check. Her teeth began to chatter, and she couldn't seem to stop shivering. Stripping off her wet clothes, she stepped into the hot shower and scrubbed herself vigorously. The strangest aspect of the entire situation was that it had been so unexpected. Shay allowed the water to pour over her, mildly surprised by the tears sliding silently down her cheeks.

Adam's deception had come as a complete shock. It hadn't crossed her mind that he'd intended to entertain another woman tonight. What a stupid, naive fool she was. His message should have been instantly decipherable—especially to her. How many times had she listened to her father's glib lies? She had never been fooled by them. Case said that the three Flynns were all "seasoned lie-catchers" because they'd been raised on them. If only she'd caught Adam's lie. She could have spent a quiet evening in her apartment, avoiding the horrendous drive through the blizzard and the most mortifying, crushing scene of her entire life!

Shay noted with surprise that her new clothes had been hung in the immense closet, her new shoes were on the shoe rack, and the lingerie was arranged neatly in the bureau drawers. Had Adam done all this? He really did have a compulsion for neatness.

She bypassed all that was new, settling on a canary-yellow nightgown—a gift from Candy accompanied by her exasperated "I'm so damn sick of purple!"—old fuzzy slippers, and trusty lilac robe. Although the thought of food held little appeal, her stomach's rumblings insisted that she was indeed hungry. Pregnancy was an extraordinary force, she mused as she padded along the hallway. She was cold and tired and wanted nothing more than to climb into bed, but her body's demand for a meal drove her into the kitchen. She dreaded another encounter with Adam and Bunny, but they were nowhere to be seen.

The animals were overjoyed with her company, and Shay fed them, then talked to them as she fixed her own supper of tomato soup and a grilled cheese sandwich. She grimaced at the sight of the unscraped dinner dishes and assortment of dirty pots and pans. Apparently Bunny's willingness to make dinner for poor, helpless Adam didn't extend to cleaning up afterward. Shay scowled at the mess as she carefully rinsed her own dishes and placed them in the dishwasher. *She* certainly wasn't going to clean up after them!

She wasn't sure when it dawned on her that she was alone in the house. When Bruno and the kittens raced through the downstairs, knocking over a plant and a lamp in the process, and there was no comment from anyone, she became curious. A quick search of the house confirmed her growing suspicions. Bunny and Adam were gone!

With enormous relief, she slipped under the enveloping warmth of the king-sized comforter. It would have been more than dreadful for the three of them to have spent the night under the same roof. Such a situation required a degree of sophistication and tolerance that she didn't possess.

Bruno's barking roused her from a deep sleep, and the sound of footsteps on the stairs catapulted her into instant awareness. Burglars? The day needed only this to immortalize itself as the worst in her life.

The bedroom door opened and a dark form crept inside. Shay decided to feign sleep, the best course of action according to a recent police survey she had read. The light in Adam's closet snapped on, and Shay angled a peek over the top of the covers.

It was Adam.

The sight of her husband peeling off his clothes sent a fresh surge of anger coursing through her veins. She climbed out of bed and headed quietly for the door.

"Shay, where are you going?" He was at her side in an instant, and she muttered an imprecation. How had he heard her? She'd been stealthy as a cat.

"I'm going to another room. I wouldn't have used this one if I'd known you were coming back."

Adam sighed. "I took Bunny home, Shay. I had every intention of coming back."

"Why?" She was annoyed with herself for asking. She didn't care what he did.

"I couldn't let Bunny stay here, and I wasn't about to stay at her place. Does that answer your question?" When she didn't reply, he continued, "Nothing happened between Bunny and me tonight, Shay. Absolutely nothing."

"Sorry about that. I guess my timing was a bit off. Next time I'll give you a few more hours."

"Dammit, Shay, why won't you let me explain? I didn't invite Bunny here, she simply arrived. She was hysterically upset. She needed a friend."

"Don't we all," Shay murmured.

Adam flexed his fingers. She had the uncomfortable feeling that he would have enjoyed wrapping them around her throat. But then, conventional, civilized Adam would never resort to such primitive tactics.

His control increased her rage. "Step aside, Adam, I'm leaving this room."

"Shay, I want you to listen to me." Adam leaned against the door, effectively blocking her passage. "Bunny and I talked about my uncle's announcement and her limited future with the firm. I tried to suggest other firms that she may want to consider. It's been a difficult day for Bunny, Shay. Her career means everything to her."

When Shay continued to stare at him impassively, he forged on. "We were both hungry, and Bunny offered to cook dinner. We spent the rest of the evening talking, waiting for the storm to let up so she could leave."

"I'm used to much better stories than that, Adam. Remember my father was Irish and he had the Gaelic gift for spinning tales."

"I'm not your father and I'm not a liar."

Shay shrugged. "It doesn't matter anyway. I don't care what you do or who you do it with."

"Not much!" Adam exploded. "I saw your expression when Bunny stepped into the hall tonight." A sudden light gleamed in his angry gray eyes. "Have you bothered to ask yourself why you're so jealous, Shay? And you are jealous—you're sick with it."

"I am not!" Shay cried, goaded beyond fury by his smug assertion. "But I am concerned about the future welfare of my baby. The minute your precious Bunny set foot in this house, you got rid of my cats and the dog, at her request. I foresee the same treatment for my child." She drew a deep, shaky breath. "I'm warning you, Adam, I'll—I'll never allow my child to be alone with you. I can't trust you. You'd probably invite your cuddly Bunny over and dispatch the baby to the cellar—or worse."

Adam paled. "That's a rotten thing to say. I didn't suspect you could be such a sharp-tongued little bitch, Shay."

"And you're a liar and a cheat." She lifted her chin proudly. She would quit now, before they escalated into an uproar reminiscent of her parents' brawls. "Good night, Adam."

"You're sleeping here tonight, Shay. With me. All night, every night." Adam effortlessly picked her up in his arms and carried her to the bed. Like a battery-operated toy triggered by his touch, Shay began to hammer against his chest with her fists and kick her legs uselessly, in a scissorslike motion.

"You're a self-centered, insensitive beast! You can't expect me to sleep with you after what's happened tonight!"

"Nothing happened tonight, Shay! Nothing has

changed since last night. You're my wife and I want to make love to you." He laid her gently on the bed. "I'm going to make love to you, Shay."

"No! I can't stand to have you touch me! I loathe you!" Shay continued to fight him until he caught both her wrists and chained them above her head with one big hand. He slung a powerful leg over both of hers, immobilizing her.

"Shay, Shay, remember last night." His lips feathered her eyelids, her cheeks, her throat. "It was wonderful, darling, you made me so happy. When I woke up this morning I wanted you again, I wanted to tell you how much last night meant to me, but you had already gone. I spent all day dreaming of you, wanting you."

"Oh, how dare you! You must think I'm an utter moron, to try to tell me *that!*" Shay struggled wildly in his grasp. "You told me to stay in town tonight, have you forgotten? You planned to spend the night with Bunny."

"I didn't! I—"

"Are you saying that you would have taken her home if I hadn't made my ill-timed arrival here tonight? Don't lie to me, Adam. You had no intention of venturing out in that storm!"

"She might have stayed here, Shay, but not with me, not in our bed. She would have used one of the other rooms."

"And if I swallow that, you'll probably try to sell me the Brooklyn Bridge! At least credit me with minimal intelligence."

"I credit you with a great deal of intelligence, Shay. What I'm asking is your understanding, your trust. I don't lie, Shay, I'm not a womanizer. I—"

"Have you ever slept with Bunny?" Her dark blue eyes glittered. "The truth, Adam."

"Shay, that has absolutely nothing to do with—"

"You're evading the question, counselor." She pinned him with a cool, Candy line. "Have you slept with her?"

"This is ridiculous. I refuse to be grilled, Shay."

"May I assume that your reluctance to answer means 'yes'?"

"All right, yes. I have, occasionally. But not tonight, Shay. Not since I married you." He cupped her chin with his hand. "Not since I married you, Shay."

"Should I congratulate you on your restraint? We've only been married three days, Adam."

"I don't want Bunny Warrington," Adam said tightly. "I don't think I ever really did. Damn, how can I make you understand? I don't understand it myself, the way I feel about you. . . ." His voice trailed off. With a sudden, alarming urgency, his mouth descended upon hers. His hand closed over her breast, his thumb flicking possessively over the nipple. "If I can't reach you with words, I'll try this," he breathed, nibbling at her throat. He pressed against her, and his hard masculine response confirmed his intentions.

Shay closed her eyes in silent misery. He was determined to win back her trust through sex, and she was certain no further argument would sway him. His masculine ego was at stake. Why fight him? she asked herself with weary resignation. He would win anyway and she would only exhaust herself further, perhaps even harm the baby in some way. She gave up the struggle and allowed him to make love to her, but most of her past responsiveness was lacking. She lay quietly beneath him, her emotions oddly detached while her body moved automatically with his. Something inside her had died tonight. The passion was gone. When Adam was finished, she rolled over on her side, relieved that it was over.

"I won't let you do it, Shay." Adam caught her round the waist and pulled her into the warm curve of his body. "I won't let you shut me out. You were hurt and tired tonight. Tomorrow—"

"Will be the same, Adam," she finished miserably.

"I don't believe that, Shay. You won't be able to hold

back for long, darling. You're too passionate, too giving, too sweet . . ."

". . . too gullible, too stupid," Shay added. "Not anymore, Adam. I realize that you expect sex in exchange for room and board, and you'll get it. But nothing more."

"I want a hell of a lot more than sex from you, Shay!" His arm around her tightened. "And I intend to get it."

"I have nothing more to give." She tried to wriggle out of his hold, but he wouldn't release her. Closing her eyes with an angry sigh, Shay lay stiffly in his arms until the emotional and physical exhaustion of the day overwhelmed her and she drifted into sleep.

The next morning the DJ on a local radio station read a long list of schools that were closed because of the severity of the previous night's storm. All District of Columbia schools were closed, along with most in the outlying suburban areas.

Shay was ambivalent about the closing. Although a day's rest was welcome, she would have preferred to immerse herself in work to forget last night's fiasco. The students would be ecstatic, she knew. An unexpected holiday was always a joy to them.

She was already dressed in jeans and a print maternity top when Adam appeared in the kitchen. He had showered and shaved and wore a three-piece navy pinstripe suit, as always the quintessential, polished urban attorney.

"There's no school today," she explained. The atmosphere between them was at once awkward, strained, and electric.

"I'm not surprised. I heard on the radio that we had more than a foot of snow last night," Adam replied politely. "The major roadways are supposed to be clear, though. The road crews worked all night. I thought I'd go into the office today—unless you'd rather I remain here with you?"

"Oh, no," Shay blurted out, a little too quickly. "That is, I'll probably paint all day. Sally Vasey is expecting those Christmas canvases." She strove for the same blandly civil tones as his. "You needn't stay here on my account. I'll be busy and I have plenty of company."

Bruno gave a cheerful bark, as if to affirm her statement. The kittens were already chasing each other madly around the kitchen. There was a moment's silence, and she asked, "Would you care for some breakfast?"

Adam smiled and sat down at the table, a copy of The *Washington Post* in his hand. "Yes, thank you, Shay. I would."

She expected him to bury himself in the newspaper, but he didn't glance at it all through breakfast. He praised the grapefruit and the rye toast and the instant coffee so effusively that her eyes narrowed in suspicion. What was he up to now? The breakfast was adequate but certainly didn't deserve a rave review.

"You're a fantastic cook, Shay," he told her for the tenth time. "That was the best breakfast I've ever eaten."

"Well, it didn't take a whole lot of talent to prepare it," she replied at last. "I daresay anyone can slice a grapefruit and put bread in the toaster and boil water. You're laying it on a bit thick, Adam."

"I'm just appreciative that you fixed breakfast for me, darling," he said huskily.

She recognized that glimmer in his eyes and quickly stepped away. She was not up for a sexy little postbreakfast scene. But Adam didn't pursue her. He reached instead for his leather attaché case.

"I guess I'll start painting now," she said. Flashing a false smile, she called to him, "Have a nice day," with all the warmth of the National Weather Service's recorded forecast.

When Adam came home that evening, Shay was still painting, and five completed needlepoint designs lay drying atop the kitchen counters.

"These are beautiful, darling. They're marvelous," he said with great enthusiasm. "You're very talented."

Shay didn't look up. "That's me. A talented painter and a fantastic cook. Care to add any other accolades?"

He leaned down to kiss the top of her head. "I can see how busy you've been all day, sweetheart. Would you like me to take you out to dinner?"

"I found some things in the freezer and put together a stew," she said, dabbing her brush into a small mound of red acrylic paint. "It's in the oven now and should be ready in about twenty minutes. Of course, if you want to go out, you needn't feel obliged to eat it."

"Go out? When I can stay home and have your terrific cooking?" Adam exclaimed heartily. "Stew, eh? So that's the wonderful aroma I smelled when I came in! Stew happens to be one of my favorite dishes, Shay."

Shay rolled her eyes heavenward. "Why is it I think you'd have said that even if I told you that I was broiling grasshoppers?"

For a moment Adam appeared nonplussed, then he began to laugh. "Broiled grasshoppers! Van was right, Shay. You really do have a great sense of humor."

She heaved a disgusted sigh. "How long are you going to keep this up, Adam? I don't believe a word you say, you know."

He didn't react angrily or defensively, as she half-expected him to. "Let's just take it one day at a time, darling," he said softly.

She read the hunger in his eyes and knew that it had nothing to do with his alleged fondness for stew. She backed away warily.

Just as quickly the longing was gone and his expression was one of indefatigable cheerfulness. "I feel like the luckiest man in the world, Shay. How many other men come home to a beautiful wife who has a delicious hot stew waiting for him in the oven? Would you like me to set the table, darling? I can't wait to taste that fabulous stew."

What a shame she hadn't oversalted it, Shay thought sourly. As it was, the stew really was delicious and she had to endure Adam's praising it and her for the rest of the evening.

Eleven

And so it continued for the rest of the week. Adam lavished praise on her every word and action; if she said or did nothing, he praised that, too. Was he trying to drive her crazy? Shay wondered, after one of her particularly caustic remarks had earned a compliment on her "terrific wit." Why was Adam treating her this way? Nothing she said or did could shake his overly kind, overly amicable demeanor, though she made great efforts to rile him.

She couldn't recall anyone ever being more eager to please her or to gratify her every whim. Adam seemed attuned to her every wish, dedicated to ensuring her comfort. He wouldn't allow her to lift a finger around the house. Maria's replacement, Janine, a cheerful young woman who loved animals, did all the laundry, cooking, and cleaning.

Plans were already underway for the conversion of a spare bedroom into a studio for her. Adam brought armfuls of wallpaper books and carpet samples home for her inspection and raved over the purple shades. He even asked if she wanted to redecorate the whole house in her favorite color. Adam Wickwire living in a purple house! Shay had stared at him, searching suspiciously for the sarcasm she knew must be behind the offer, only to find Adam smiling expectantly at her. Unless she was being exceptionally obtuse, his offer appeared to be genuine. Nevertheless, she refused the offer, too confused even to try to resume her perusal of the samples at hand.

All her belongings had been moved from her apartment, and her large collection of plants were adapting to new windows and new hooks from the ceiling, obligingly affixed by Adam. She needed only to ask to receive . . . anything.

Shay was well aware that he had refused a plethora of invitations to Christmas parties after she'd refused to attend any of them with him. Her baiting remarks about Bunny's presence at these parties drew no reaction from him, other than a sincere, "I'd rather stay home with you, sweetheart."

So they spent their evenings quietly at home together, he reading while she painted. He even suffered through her choice of record albums. "I like the Oak Ridge Boys," Adam remarked one night as she flipped the disc to its other side. "Their music has a message." He declined to reveal what the message was.

They often took Bruno for long walks over the snow-covered grounds, then warmed themselves in front of a crackling fire in the stone-and-brick fireplace. In keeping with the winter idyll, Adam even produced bags of marshmallows on a few such occasions, and they toasted them on long steel skewers.

It was almost as if he were courting her, Shay mused, but of course that could never be. Why would he bother? She was already his wife, soon she would give birth to his child, and that and his sexual desire for her were the only reasons he had married her.

Adam was simply trying to be polite. He was, after all, ever the gentleman. He would expect to coexist in peace, with sexual rapport thrown in as his eventual reward, and was willing to pacify her to achieve it.

Granted this theory had its flaws, but Shay could come up with no other. And whatever Adam's motivations, she was determined not to fall under his spell.

But it was becoming harder and harder to maintain her cool reserve. On Friday evening he presented her with the keys to a brand-new Buick. An orchid one.

"Custom paint job," he said with a grin. "Do you like it, honey?"

Shay was speechless. She'd never had a new car of her own; the old Buick was a hand-me-down from Case. And Adam had specifically ordered one in her favorite color! Buying purple cars couldn't be a Wickwire tradition. She stared at him, overwhelmed.

"Would you have preferred another make?" Adam asked anxiously. "Are you tired of Buicks? We can always get—"

"I love it! It's wonderful!" Impulsively, Shay flung her arms around his neck. It was the first real physical contact between them in days, since the evening of the Bunny debacle. Although they continued to share the bedroom, the king-sized bed was large enough that the two need never touch. And they hadn't.

"I'm glad you like it, Shay." Adam held her tightly, his face buried in the hollow of her neck. She moved slightly and her cheek brushed his. Her heart did a peculiar little somersault. He was going to kiss her. . . .

Adam released her and opened the car door with a flourish. "Let's try it out, Shay. How about driving to Angelo's for pizza?"

Shay slid behind the wheel, resolutely denying that she was disappointed by his too-brief embrace.

"Fasten your seat belt, sweetheart." He leaned across to make certain her belt was secured. His hand brushed her breast, and a bolt of fire flashed through her. She thought she heard Adam draw a deep breath, but when she stole a glance at him, he was busy with his own seat belt, his face hidden from her.

"I set the dial on that country station you like so much," he remarked in a smooth, bland tone as he switched on the radio. The voice of the late Patsy Cline filled the car with the song "Crazy," a country classic. Shay felt as if she were living the lyrics.

The next day a dozen long-stemmed red roses arrived at the house for her.

"We decided to get married one week ago today," Adam reminded her. "Tomorrow is our first anniversary, darling."

A number of snide, caustic remarks immediately sprang to mind, but Shay didn't utter one of them. In truth, she was thrilled with the roses. No one had ever sent her flowers before. It was exciting and romantic.

No. Shay quickly took herself to task. Not romantic. Whatever Adam's motives, she could definitely rule out romance. This morning she had awakened to find herself in his half of the bed, nestled warmly against him. They had kissed, long and languorously, but when Shay would have welcomed further intimacies, Adam had sprung from the bed, snatched his sweatsuit, and announced his intention to jog five miles.

They spent all Saturday afternoon together, first dropping off the completed needlepoint designs at Sally Vasey's, then shopping in Georgetown.

Shay returned home with a three-pound box of Godiva chocolates, a German music box with exquisitely carved little angels circling a Christmas tree to the tune of "O Tannenbaum," an encyclopedia, *Infancy and Early Childhood,* and six silk scarves. All gifts from Adam.

They went to The Four Seasons Hotel in Washington that night for dinner and danced afterward.

"We haven't danced together since that night in Casey's apartment," Adam murmured huskily, holding her tightly against his long, hard body.

"No, we haven't." Shay sighed. It was wonderful being in his arms again, she acknowledged achingly. She wrapped herself around him and closed her eyes.

"You look beautiful tonight, Shay," Adam whispered, his lips caressing her neck.

She was wearing one of her new maternity outfits, a full-cut chemise-style dress in lavender, pink, and gray. Adam had insisted that she wear her hair down, and he tangled his fingers in the thick sable tresses. "Your hair is like silk," His voice was husky. "Gorgeous."

Shay didn't want to hear it. He'd been complimenting her nonstop for the past week; she was tired of words. She wanted . . . she gazed limpidly into his eyes, his beautiful, slate-gray eyes. She felt as if she were being drawn into them, into him. The way he was looking at her made her feel weak and hot. Oh, his mouth. She wanted him to kiss her so badly.

The half-formed thoughts were erased entirely by the firm pressure of Adam's mouth on hers. It was like lighting a match to an already smoldering fire. Shay was engulfed by the wild flames of desire that licked through her veins. She forgot that they were in the middle of a crowded dance floor, forgot the horrible scene with Bunny Warrington, forgot everything but her hunger and need for her husband. She molded herself to him, pressing the soft contours of her body into the hard masculine planes of his.

"Easy, sweetheart." Adam gently disengaged himself from her. "I think we'd better sit down."

She was trembling as he guided her back to the table.

"I want to go home," she said, and he immediately motioned to the waiter for the check.

Shay was a bundle of nerves during the drive back to Potomac. Would he try to make love to her? And if he did, should she capitulate reluctantly or at once? She had no doubt that she would surrender to him. She wanted him too much not to. By the time Adam pulled the car into the circular driveway, Shay had formulated her strategy.

For her pride's sake, she couldn't allow him to sweep her instantly into bed. She would allow him to kiss her, then demur. However, she would not pull out of his arms. She would cuddle provocatively close and whisper, "No." Of course he would overrule her.

He didn't! The kiss was lingering and hot and deep, all Shay had been dreaming of. Adam swept her into his arms and carried her upstairs to their bedroom.

"Darling." He laid her gently down on the bed and kissed her again. "I want to make love to you, Shay."

The planned scenario nearly floated out of her head as she looked into the burning gray depths of his eyes. She remembered as he was removing her dress.

"No, Adam," she demurred, clinging closely to him. Her voice was barely a whisper.

"Shay," Adam murmured, almost to himself as she raised her face for his persuasive kiss that would "change her mind."

"All right, honey." He stood up abruptly, leaving her alone and stunned on the bed. "I understand. I think Bruno needs a good run outside anyway." She watched him change into his infernal jogging suit. "I'll be back shortly."

While he was gone, Shay dove into the box of chocolates. She gobbled down ten pieces and promptly felt nauseated. When he returned, Adam couldn't have been more solicitous.

They went to see *The Nutcracker* ballet at the Kennedy Center for the Performing Arts the next evening. Adam held her hand throughout the entire performance. When they returned home he presented her with a colorful, handcrafted nutcracker in the shape of a soldier, just like the one they had seen in the ballet. A memento of the evening, their one-week anniversary, he said.

Shay thanked him with a chaste kiss on his cheek and swiftly moved away from him. Having thrown herself at him the night before, only to have him reject her to walk the dog, she was not about to repeat her mistake.

On Monday morning a dozen white roses arrived in the art room at school along with a card signed simply, "Adam." He arrived home that evening with a dozen more of the same. On Tuesday there were two dozen yellow roses delivered to the art room.

The students were amazed.

"I gotta meet this guy." Chandra inhaled the roses' scent with an appreciative sigh.

"Is he a florist or something?" Anthony wanted to know.

He was driving her to distraction, Shay thought wildly, returning home to find a mixed bouquet of purple flowers waiting for her. He'd even agreed to go caroling with the Art Club the following week and treat them all to pizza afterward.

Why was he doing it? she asked herself over and over again. Anyone witnessing the way he pampered her, the way he babied and indulged her, would think that he adored her. Shay knew it couldn't be so. She came up with yet another theory.

Adam's generosity and charming attentiveness must merely be a sop because he no longer desired her. Of course! Her advancing pregnancy had turned him off, and since he'd only wanted her physically to begin with, whatever feelings he had for her were now dead. But, being a Wickwire and a gentleman, he couldn't bring himself to actively repulse a pregnant woman, so he tried to divert her with gifts and compliments.

She should be happy, Shay admonished herself. She'd never wanted to become involved in a heavy sexual relationship. She hadn't wanted emotional involvement either. Except . . . all her intentions had backfired and she was already involved with Adam. More than "involved." A lot more. She was in love with him.

The realization had struck with full force one evening as she'd glanced up from her painting to find him deeply engrossed in a book. She had studied the curve of his mouth, the serious slate-gray eyes, and her heart had blazed. She loved him. She had loved him for weeks, probably since their very first weekend together, and hadn't recognized her feelings as love.

She wanted to spend her life with him. She knew in that instant that their life together needn't be the nightmare her parents' had been. She wondered why she had ever thought it would. She and Adam were as different from her parents as their child's life would be from hers. But . . .

The week rolled on. Shay's acknowledgment of her love for Adam made his kind overtures even harder to resist. There was a bittersweet pain in accepting his attentions, knowing they weren't based on the love she wished he possessed for her. Confused and unhappy, Shay withdrew further, her protective walls keeping Adam at bay.

Her apprehension grew as Saturday and the anticipated arrival of Adam's family drew near. She was certain the Wickwires would dislike her on sight. Why shouldn't they? She wasn't of their world and she had displaced Bunny Warrington, who was.

She didn't dare voice her fears to Adam. She couldn't confide in him, for he already found her lacking. Her pride demanded that she keep up a facade of cool indifference. Shay took some small measure of satisfaction in the fact that Adam didn't know how very much she was dreading this weekend.

Adam's sister, Pierce Prescott Wickwire Sloan (Bitsy), and her husband, Jonathan Charles (J.C.), were scheduled to arrive first. Adam drove to the airport to pick them up while Shay waited nervously back at the house.

The elder Wickwires were driving up from Charlottesville and had expected to be in around two o'clock. They pulled up to the house three hours early, just after Adam's phone call reporting that the Sloans' flight from New York had been delayed.

Thus an unsuspecting Shay, wearing maternity jeans that were already paint-splattered and an old sweat shirt of Casey's, greeted her in-laws at the door. Each viewed the other with trepidation. The judge and his wife, Elizabeth, were as meticulously groomed as their son always was. Not even the two-and-a-half-hour car trip had wrinkled their wool suits, hers in a herringbone tweed, his in charcoal gray.

Shay, who had been painting to fill a rush order received the day before from Sally Vasey, flipped her long braid over her shoulder and wished she could sink through the earth.

"You're not Shay?" Elizabeth Wickwire asked hopefully.

Shay assured her that she was and was tempted to offer a few words of condolence to the older woman.

Conversation was rather difficult, although all three made a valiant effort. They seemed to have nothing in common. The elder Wickwires were avid participants in the fox hunts in the Virginia hunt country; Shay, born and raised in the city of Detroit, had never been near a live horse. Although Libby Wickwire professed an interest in needlepoint, she was disappointed to learn that Shay designed but did not stitch the canvases. Neither Wickwire had ever set foot in a public school; they were surprised to learn that art classes were offered there. The topic of the baby was assiduously avoided. They discussed the weather for a long, long time.

When the florists and caterers began arriving to prepare for the party that night, Shay was totally flummoxed. Adam's small gathering for the family and a few friends had grown into a full-scale event for one hundred guests. There was to be a buffet dinner at ten. Waitresses would circulate during the early part of the evening with trays of hot hors d'oeuvres; there would be two bartenders, and many drink waiters. A piano player had been hired to alternate with a small combo, so that continuous music would be provided throughout the evening. Everyone had questions to ask, and Shay had none of the answers. Her experience supervising the Art Club parties and sitting in the kitchen chatting with Candy's caterers had not prepared her to oversee an operation of this scale.

Fortunately Libby Wickwire *did* have the experience. She—who had done elaborate entertaining at home all her years, who could chair balls for five hundred couples without turning a hair—did consider an intimate little Christmas party for a hundred people mere child's play. After the initial shock at learning that Shay had never given a party, Libby took over, assuming command like a general on a battlefield. She knew where the florist should place his arrangements, where the extra chairs that had been rented should go, what to advise the caterers and bartenders on placement of their wares. Shay was awed.

"Adam loves to entertain," his mother confided, "and he does it often."

"How often?" Shay asked uneasily. She was overwhelmed by the number of people in the house, the constant comings and goings of vans and trucks, bringing everything from bags of ice to extra tables.

"Oh, he likes to throw big parties at least twice a year," Libby replied blithely.

At that point Judge Wickwire took Bruno out for a walk and his wife ordered the kittens to the basement. Shay didn't dare contradict her. The greedy little cats were already circling a vat of shrimp with predatory menace.

"If you don't mind, I'll shower and change," Shay said when she managed to catch her mother-in-law between conferences with the piano player and the chef.

She dressed with the care one might exert when dressing for a State dinner, choosing a dark plaid maternity jumper with a navy jersey and tights. She brushed her hair until it shone, securing it on her crown with two tortoiseshell barrettes.

The table was set and the lunch ready when Adam, Bitsy, and J.C. finally arrived.

"Sorry for the delay, darling." Adam slipped an arm around Shay's shoulders and kissed her lightly, his hand wandering to the curve of her neck. "But things seem to be well under way here." He stroked her nape with gentle fingers. "And you look lovely as always, sweetheart."

His family watched Adam's display of husbandly affection with interest. Shay bit back the urge to tell them that it *was* merely a display, that Adam had not betrayed his upbringing in his dealings with his wife, that he was, as ever, a first-class gentleman.

The afternoon passed slowly. Adam's mother was clearly in her element as she immersed herself in the endless details of the party. Bitsy spent most of the afternoon talking on the phone to her innumerable friends in the area. The three men retired to the den and discussed the stock market, then economic conditions in general.

Shay wandered through the house, unsure of what to do with herself. It seemed antisocial to shut herself away in the bedroom cum studio and paint, and she was superfluous to the party preparations, Bitsy's phone calls, and the discussion in the den.

She visited the kittens in the basement for a while, walked the dog, and finally announced that she was going upstairs to nap. It seemed an acceptable excuse for a pregnant woman and she spent several pleasant hours reading magazines and dozing in her bedroom. Oddly enough, she reflected, she didn't feel the least bit guilty about not being busy, productive, helpful. Then it was time to start to dress for the Big Event: her first party as Adam Wickwire's wife.

Twelve

"I guess throwing this party wasn't one of my better ideas," Adam admitted ruefully to Shay as they viewed the laughing, drinking, glittering crowd that packed the downstairs of their home. "The numbers somehow got out of hand, but I couldn't bring myself to slight anyone."

"And no one wanted to miss the show," Shay replied tersely. "I've heard people bowed out of other engagements to attend this party of yours, Adam. How nice that you have one hundred very close friends. Most people have only two or three, some less than that." Shay couldn't keep the tart remarks to herself any longer.

"I had that one coming." Adam sighed. "We should have spent a simple and quiet weekend with my parents. I realize that now, Shay."

"And miss all the hilarious jokes about Planned Parenthood and ten-pound premature babies? All the nudges and winks and innuendos? Your friends are having a marvelous time! Think of all the fun we would have denied them, Adam."

"They don't mean to be malicious, Shay. But some

of my old friends and I have kidded each other for years, about everything and anything. We—"

"Well, they're certainly getting a lot of mileage out of your 'hasty' marriage. And seeing your bride in a maternity dress has inspired them to dizzying heights of bad taste."

Adam groaned. "I'm sorry, sweetheart. They mean no harm, really, but I should have guessed that it would be . . . well, difficult for you."

"Oh, I love being the object of aging preppies' ribald humor. I'm having a wonderful time, Adam."

"Shay, please!" Adam was miserable.

The jokes hadn't bothered her *that* much, and there were far fewer than she had expected. She knew there was no real malevolence involved, and open teasing probably was the best way to handle this unorthodox situation. Still, she couldn't seem to stop needling Adam. He was being ridiculously overprotective toward her, flinching at each and every rejoinder tossed their way.

"Sweetheart, I never wanted you to be hurt." He sounded anguished, and Shay nearly smiled. She had never been one to have her feelings easily bruised. Actually, some of the remarks made by Adam's old prep-school friends struck her as quite witty. But she was enjoying Adam's loss of his cool composure and control. If only he knew that *he* was the person with the power to really hurt her! She relented and patted his arm in consolation.

"Why, there's David Falk and Paulette Wilder," she said, surprised to see them together.

Adam leaped on the remark, one of the few non-barbed ones she had directed to him all evening. "Paulette's wrapped around him like a clinging vine. She's making certain that she has his attention tonight."

"She might just snare him yet," Shay commented dryly.

Adam leaned over to brush her temple with his lips. "Would you like another ginger ale, honey? More hors d'oeuvres?" he asked solicitously. His hand curved possessively over her hip, as it had all evening. He hadn't left her side since the arrival of the first guests. He was playing the role of devoted bridegroom and father-to-be to the hilt.

"Nothing, thank you." Shay searched the room for a glimpse of her sister. Candy had arrived early with a distinguished-looking, silver-haired gentleman in tow. He was a well-known defense attorney, currently in town for a criminal case. Shay knew that Candy had maintained a casual relationship with him for the past few years. Predictably, Case had been unable to come tonight. He was on call at the hospital, he'd explained. Predictably. Case was always on call.

"Adam! Shay!" Catherine Bennington, lovely in burgundy velvet, enfolded both Adam and Shay in an excited embrace. "I'm taking full credit for this, you know."

"Catherine has told everyone that she introduced you two." Bill Bennington smiled indulgently at his wife. "She's ready to hang out her matchmaker's shingle."

"Shay, you look wonderful." Catherine surveyed her with an almost maternal pride.

Shay thanked her politely. For the first time in her life she was wearing a dress with a three figure price-tag. A deceptively simple creation in royal blue, the dress, a designer original, proclaimed status to every woman in the room. Adam had brought it home for her the day before, along with the exquisite sapphire-and-diamond earrings she also wore tonight.

"You do look beautiful, darling," Adam said for the twentieth time that night. Or was it the twenty-first? Shay thanked him as politely as she had thanked Catherine.

The Benningtons moved on, and Adam turned once more to Shay. "Is the crowd too much for you, honey? Do you feel all right?"

"Don't worry, I'm not going to faint," Shay replied, humor lighting her dark blue eyes. "That was the entertainment at Candy's party. I don't like to repeat myself."

"It's been two weeks since that party." Adam's voice was low and suggestive. "I first learned that you were carrying my child two weeks ago tonight. It's changed my life, Shay. I've—"

"Mine, too," Shay said sadly. Marriage to Adam had shown her that she could never be truly happy without him. The thought depressed her beyond measure. "I wish we could turn back the clock to that Saturday. I'd follow my first inclination and stay away from Candy's party."

"Well, we can't undo what's been done," Adam snapped in the first display of temper since she'd found him with Bunny Warrington that terrible Tuesday night. "We're married, Shay, and this party is a celebration of that fact."

"Yes, rather like the wake following the funeral."

"Can we dispense with the cute comebacks? I've really had enough of them for one night."

"Aren't you going to rave about my great wit, my irrepressible sense of humor?" Shay was delighted she had irritated him and tried to hide her grin. Genuine anger was preferable to his expansive cordiality of the past ten days.

Adam glanced down at her, his gray eyes assessing her. "For one who has been practically catatonic most of the day, you seem to be getting rather feisty, Shay. What gives?"

Before she could answer, Bunny Warrington, her clingy black dress sporting a plunging neckline and no back, was upon them, her lovely mouth contorted into an unlovely grimace. Shay took an instinctive step back, loathing the prospect of another scene. That Tuesday night's confrontation had been enough melodrama to last her a lifetime.

"Adam, may I speak with you?" Bunny asked huskily, laying a hand on the soft cashmere of his jacket sleeve. "I'll only take a moment of your time." Her pale eyes glistened with unshed tears, and Adam was immediately solicitous.

"What is it, Bunny?"

"I shouldn't have come tonight, Adam." Bunny's eyes locked with Adam's. "I knew people would be talking; I've been fielding questions all week. But for appearance' sake . . ." She smiled wanly, looking fragile and distressed—and very beautiful. "Oh, I was coping beautifully until—until—" Bunny broke off, seemingly unable to go on.

Despite her dismay, Shay couldn't help but admire the ingenuity of the other woman's ploy. Her vulnerability was incredibly appealing, and Adam the gentleman would respond as he had been trained to do. With masculine sympathy and concern.

"Until what, Bunny?" he asked gently.

One perfectly shaped teardrop slid from the corner of Bunny's eye. Shay thought of her own bouts of weeping, complete with red eyes and stuffed nose. How did Bunny manage it?

"Your uncle has been cordial to me tonight, of course, but there's a definite coolness in his attitude that hurts, Adam," Bunny whimpered. "I'm willing to admit that I let the firm down in the Morrison case, but to be treated as a pariah—"

"Bunny, you've got to stop flagellating yourself," Adam interrupted. "You are a fine attorney. You can't let an unfortunate lapse ruin your confidence and career."

Shay shifted uncomfortably, feeling like the proverbial third wheel. Adam removed his hand from her hip to place it reassuringly on Bunny's forearm.

Bunny smiled wanly. "Adam, the final straw tonight came when I saw Bill Prescott approach your sister-in-law with the enthusiasm of a groupie greeting a rock star. I—I actually heard him make her an offer to join Wickwire, Prescott & Sinclair."

"I'm sure he was only joking, Bunny," Adam replied, but thunderclouds were gathering in his gray eyes.

"There is often truth in jest, Adam," Bunny whispered, moving closer. "And there's a certain logic in it all. The firm is weakest in her area of expertise. Oh, Adam, I do want to stay with the firm. I can't believe your uncle really means to hold my advancement to a standstill, but if *she*'s there, if Candace Flynn joins Wickwire, Prescott & Sinclair . . ."

"She won't," Adam and Shay chorused; Adam threatening, Shay encouraging. Candy would never give up her lucrative independent practice to join a conservative, business-oriented firm.

But the mere suggestion of it appeared to have enraged Adam. "Let's have a little talk with my uncle, Bunny. I want to make it clear that . . ." His voice trailed off as he and Bunny walked away from Shay. They had both forgotten her in their mutual moment of crisis.

Shay watched them go, her mind assessing the situation. So Adam had been telling the truth that night when he'd mentioned his uncle's threats about Bunny's position in the firm. She really hadn't believed him until this moment. And if he'd been telling the truth about that, perhaps he also hadn't lied when he'd said that Bunny's visit was not prearranged. That meant that he hadn't told her to remain in town so that he could enjoy a tryst with his lovely colleague.

But the point was moot now. Adam hadn't made love to her for nearly two weeks. The ease with which he withdrew from her made it painfully clear that he didn't want or desire her anymore.

Shay took a stuffed mushroom from the tray of a smiling waitress, who weaved her way in and out of the crowd, proferring goodies. When would this party, this evening, ever end?

"Shay, your brother's on the phone and wants to talk to your sister." Janine, the housekeeper, provided a welcome interruption of Shay's melancholy thoughts a few minutes later. "Would you like to find her or take the call?"

"I'll take the call," Shay said instantly, glad for the excuse to leave the party. She slipped upstairs to her bedroom and picked up the blue receiver. "Case? What's wrong?" Her brother wouldn't call Candy at a party unless some emergency warranted it.

"I want to talk to Candy, love. Would you get her for me?" As always, Casey Flynn would attempt to shield his baby sister from any unpleasantness. Shay decided it was high time to break that pattern.

"Tell me what's the matter, Case," she said sternly.

"There's no need to involve you in this, little one," Case said in a low, sweet tone of voice.

"I'm not a little one, Casey Flynn," Shay said, bristling. "I'm twenty-eight years old, a married woman who will soon be a mother, and I demand to know what's going on."

Case heaved a sigh. "Dad's in town, Shay. He was picked up this morning for passing bad checks. Bail has been set, and I was on my way over to the jail to get him out, when one of my patients took a turn for the worse."

"Dad's in jail?" Shay gasped.

"In the D.C. jail," Case affirmed. "I can't leave this patient, Shay. There's a possibility that we might have to do surgery within the hour. I was going to ask Candy to stop by the hospital to get the money and bail Dad out tonight."

Shay thought of her sister with her current lover, the criminal-defense lawyer. "Poor Candy. For her to go to the jail to bail out her own father . . . Oh, Case, she's an attorney! She'll be humiliated."

"True. She's going to have a fit, but we've got to get him out of jail as soon as possible. If he stays overnight, he'll just get into more trouble. Last year, in the Vegas jail, he tried to bribe a guard and assaulted another prisoner. God, Candy is going to flip. When she bailed him out in Atlantic City last month, she warned him to stay out of trouble if he ever came to D.C. I don't think he was in town for an hour before he got himself arrested."

Shay felt sick. "He—he's been in jail before? How many times, Case? And why wasn't I ever told?"

"Honey, the old man's been bouncing in and out of jail for years. Candy and I take turns bailing him out. It's my turn this time. And we've never told you because you've always been so sensitive, Shay. Too sensitive about Mother and Dad." He drew a deep breath. "Don't let the news traumatize you, Shay. Dad will never change, but the way he lives his life has nothing to do with you or Candy or me and our lives."

Shay was too shocked to speak. All these years her sister and brother had been protecting her from this knowledge, bearing the shame and the expense alone. She'd long been aware of her father's gambling and womanizing, but to learn that he had a criminal record . . . It was time she grew up and faced reality, as Candy and Case had. It was time, she decided at that moment, to take her turn and assume part of the burden from her sister and brother.

"I'll go to the jail and bail him out, Case," she said firmly. At least she could spare Candy that humiliation.

"You'd rather go to jail than hang around your party, hmmm?" Case joked in an attempt at gallow's humor. "I've already got the cash, Shay. Just stop by the hospital on your way."

"I—I'll need directions to the jail, too." Shay tried a little gallows humor of her own. "It isn't one of my everyday stops."

"I'll have the directions for you, sweetie. See you soon."

It would be easy to slip away unnoticed, Shay thought as she rummaged through her purse for her car keys. Adam and Candy and the other Wickwires were lost in the crowd of strangers. No matter. She had no intention of telling any of them that she was leaving.

She felt such shame, such shock and humiliation. Case was probably right—she was too sensitive about her parents' flaws. But a criminal record in her family was a disgrace that would drive the Wickwires straight up the wall. Poor Adam, with his wife from the wrong side of the tracks and a petty crook for a father-in-law. He didn't deserve such a stigma!

The D.C. jail was located on the grounds of the sprawling complex of buildings that comprised D.C. General Hospital in southeast Washington. Shay parked the orchid Buick and walked into the imposing stone edifice like one in a dream.

She paid the bondsman and waited for her father to be brought out of the lockup, numbed by a queer sense of unreality. She had never been near a jail in her life, and here she was, bailing her own father out of one. It was such a dismal, oppressive place; she felt as if she were floundering in a nightmare.

"Shay!" Her father greeted her jauntily, waving to her across the waiting room. He was a handsome man, with the deep, dark blue eyes of the Flynns and a full head of dark hair, just beginning to turn silver. When he reached her side, he swept her up in a bear hug. "This is my baby girl, Shay Kathleen. A little darlin', with her papa's Irish blue eyes," he boasted grandly to the police officer accompanying him.

Shay couldn't look at the officer. "Let's get out of here, Dad," she said grimly, snatching her father's arm. He allowed her to lead him from the jailhouse to her car, all the while indulging in a cheerful, nonstop monologue.

"I'm taking you to Casey's place," she told him when she could get a word in. "He said you could spend the night there, but he's putting you on a plane first thing tomorrow morning. And—and we don't want you back in town until the court date. Candy will find a lawyer to handle your case." There! She had delivered her brother's message, word for word.

"I hope he's sending me someplace warm." Michael

Flynn was obviously unperturbed by the orders to leave town. "Florida is great this time of year."

Shay drove in silence, suppressing the fury that burned within her. How, she wondered in a kind of desperate rage, could she and Case and Candy be related to this person?

"So what have you been doing with yourself, my darlin' girl?" Michael asked heartily, sounding for all the world a doting father.

"I'm married," Shay replied flatly. "I'm going to have a baby."

Her father seemed delighted with the news, although she had long learned to discount anything he said. "I want to start the wee one out right, Shay. I'll play the numbers of his birth date and give him the winnings if it hits."

Shay laughed in spite of herself. What a diverse pair of grandfathers her child would have. One would bequeath the respected Wickwire name, the other his possible winnings on a number.

Thinking of Judge Wickwire sobered her instantly. Judges sentenced criminals; they did not share grandchildren with them! She left her father at Casey's apartment with a promise to inform him of the baby's birth and drove onto the Beltway, knowing that she wasn't going to return home. Not yet.

She desperately needed to talk, and the one person she knew who would not be shocked or scandalized by her father's criminal record was her friend Paul Deroy. He was accepting and nonjudgmental. In the years he had been at Carver High he had never expressed horror at any of the students' backgrounds, and some of them were hair-raising.

Paul was home, as she had prayed he would be. He was astonished to see her, but welcomed her warmly and without question. They sat in his small living room, he with hot coffee, she with cocoa, and Shay hesitantly began to tell him of the night's revelations.

The master's degree Paul had earned in counseling

had included many courses in psychology, and he seemed to understand what motivated a Michael Flynn. He spoke of a limited capacity to care deeply for others and an underdeveloped conscience. A character disorder, he diagnosed; one that would never change.

"A disorderly character," Shay corrected, smiling grimly.

"You have to learn to let go of the past, Shay," Paul said, hinting at the unspoken. "You can't judge others on the basis of your experience with your folks. Your parents were limited and untrustworthy, but—" He was interrupted by the shrill ring of the telephone. As he rose to answer it, he knocked over his half-full coffee cup. The dark brown liquid made a dramatic contrast to the pale gold fabric of the sofa.

"Sponge it quickly with cold water," Shay suggested. "I'll get the phone."

Paul was soaking the spot with ice water when she returned. "There was no one on the line," she said as she helped battle the stain. "Probably some of our dear students enjoying a prank call."

After that, conversation shifted to the general: school, the students, the coming holidays, the Art Club caroling party.

"You're a married lady now." Paul smiled wistfully. "I guess I won't get that kiss under the mistletoe this year."

"Of course you will." Warmth coursed through Shay. Paul had been so kind to her tonight. She was deeply grateful for his friendship, and it was those combined feelings of gratitude and friendship that drove her to put her arms around him. "You'll get it early and without the mistletoe." Smiling, she touched her lips lightly to his cheek.

Paul's arms encircled her at once, and he turned his head to capture her lips with his. Shay gasped a protest that was quickly smothered by his mouth. The kiss was long and hard, full of his pent-up frustration and longing. Shay abandoned her initial attempt to struggle, instinctively realizing that passivity was the wiser course of action. She wasn't afraid of Paul, nor did she want to hurt him by actively repulsing him. She would wait until he finished and make light of his impulse.

Seconds later, Paul lifted his head and surveyed her with a rueful expression. "I'm sorry, Shay. I had no right. I guess I got a little carried away."

She moved out of his arms, relieved there would be no hurtful scene. "Paul, I—" She was interrupted by a heavy thump at the door. Followed by another and another.

"I know you're in there, Shay!" came a roar that paid no heed to the lateness of the hour or the other tenants in the building. "Open this door or I'll break it in."

"It's Adam!" Shay gasped.

There was another forceful thud, and Shay rushed to open the door. "Adam, what are you—"

He pushed her aside and stormed into the apartment, his gray eyes glittering dangerously. "Get your coat, Shay. I'm taking you home!"

Shay had seen Adam angry before, but never like this. The rage he had exhibited upon learning of his impending fatherhood couldn't hold a candle to the explosive fury that gripped him now. He made a lunge for Paul, who neatly sidestepped him. "I ought to take you apart, Deroy. Damn it, I'm *going* to take you apart!"

"Adam!" Shay caught his arm, horrified. "What's gotten into you?"

"We seem to have a little misunderstanding here," Paul said nervously, backing away from Adam. "Shay, I think you'd better explain."

"She doesn't have to explain," Adam growled. "She left me to come to you." Glaring fiercely, he reached out to touch Shay's tousled hair. "Her hair's mussed up, her lipstick's smeared. I know exactly what was going on here, and by God, I'll have your head for it!"

"Adam, stop it!" Shay's heart was pounding with

fear, but she clutched tighter with her restraining hand. This wild-eyed beast was not the rational, controlled Adam Wickwire she thought she knew. "It's not what you think. Paul and I were just talking and—"

"Talking! Ha! Get your coat, lady. I'll deal with you after I've taken care of him."

"You'll do no such thing!" Shay positioned herself in front of Paul and glared up at her husband. "I've spent the evening discussing criminal behavior and I'm not about to witness it. I'm ashamed of you, Adam. You're not acting like a gentleman or like a lawyer."

"Now, that is rich." Adam laughed harshly. "I find my wife making love with another man and she berates me for not acting the part of gentleman-lawyer."

"We were not making love. I kissed Paul once in a gesture of friendship." She declined to elaborate on Paul's impulsive, impassioned kiss. "He was a great help to me tonight and—" She broke off abruptly. "How did you know I was here?"

"You answered the phone when I called," Adam snarled. "When I discovered you were missing from the party, your sister gave me a list of your friends' names. Deroy, here, was at the top of the list."

"Shay was upset about her father," Paul interjected quickly. "She wanted to talk and, uh, you were tied up with the party."

"You left the party to talk to Deroy about your father?" Adam snapped. "What kind of a tale is that, Shay?"

"It's as plausible as Bunny Warrington's arriving at your door in the middle of a blizzard to discuss the threats to her career made by your uncle." Shay shot that sentence at him. Then she squared her shoulders and raised her chin in defiance . . . and dread. "I had to bail my father out of the D.C. jail tonight, Adam. I drove him to Casey's place and then I came here. I . . . I just couldn't face the party after that."

She waited for Adam's horrified reaction to the news of her father's imprisonment. When it didn't come, she forged on, determined to tell the whole, sordid truth. "My father has a rap sheet a mile long, Adam. He's a confirmed crook and he has no intention of reforming. Ever. Case and Candy and I will probably be bailing him out of jails until he does something serious enough to be put away for good."

Thirteen

Shay braced herself for the condemnation, the distaste.

Adam stared from Paul to Shay, his expression enigmatic. "You went to the jail alone, and then you came here, to talk to him." His voice was toneless, giving away nothing.

"It's getting late, Shay," Paul said quietly, handing her her coat. "Why don't you go home and talk this over with your husband? I think he'll understand more than you give him credit for."

Adam hustled her out of the apartment, scarcely giving her time to call a brief good-bye to Paul. The Porsche was parked near the building, and he bundled her into the front seat without a word. Turning the key in the ignition, he gunned the motor and pulled out of the lot with a sudden burst of speed.

"Exactly what am I supposed to understand?" His words were clipped, staccato jabs. "Your urge to run to another man? Your complete inability to trust me or confide in me? Why didn't you tell me where you were going tonight, Shay? Why?"

Shay cast a glance at him. He seemed more upset

that she'd left the party without telling him than over the shocking revelation of her father's record. The notion confused her. "It never occurred to me to tell you that I was going to the jail," she said truthfully.

"Why not? I'm your husband. I should be the first one you turn to with a problem." He gripped the steering wheel more tightly. "When are you going to stop running away from me, withdrawing from me?"

Shay stared at him, nonplussed. What did any of this have to do with the really important issue at hand? "But Adam, my father is a common criminal, the type *your* father hands down sentences to. He's a jailbird, Adam."

"I don't care if he's Bluebeard, Shay, I—"

"Adam, you're a Wickwire," she felt compelled to remind him. "You have standards, certain expectations that must be met. Remember what you told me about the privileges and responsibilities of being a Wickwire?"

"You're driving me crazy!" Adam snapped. "Haven't you been listening to what I've been trying to say?"

The Porsche ground to a halt in the parking lot of a Holiday Inn. Shay stayed up at the green-and-yellow sign in bewilderment. "Why are we stopping here?"

"There were approximately forty people at the house when I left, and I assume at least half of them are still there. We're spending the night—or what's left of it—right here, Shay."

"But—but I don't have a toothbrush," was all she could stammer. "Or a nightgown."

Adam grinned. "You won't be needing the nightgown, at least. Come along, Shay."

Ten minutes later they were in a room that featured the standard adjoining bath, color television set, telephone, and Bible—plus one double bed. Adam locked the door. "Get undressed, Shay."

She stared at him.

"Or maybe I'll undress you." He caught her around the waist and anchored her to his side while he tugged at the zipper of her dress with his other hand. "Yes, this is much better."

His lips brushed the nape of her neck as he slipped the dress from her shoulders and pushed it to the floor. Her ice-blue slip and panty hose were the next to go. It happened so quickly that it took Shay several moments to gather her scattered wits. When she did, she pulled away from him, her cheeks hot. "Why are you doing this, Adam?" She chewed her lower lip anxiously. "If you're trying to humiliate me . . ."

If he was trying to humiliate her, he had succeeded admirably. She felt incredibly helpless and vulnerable standing before him in her lacy demi-cup ice-blue bra and matching panties.

"Humiliate you?" Adam laughed hoarsely. "You have an uncanny ability to misinterpret my every word and action. I'm going to make love to you, Shay."

Tears stung her eyes. So this was the way he planned to avenge himself? A quick tumble in a motel to underscore his contempt for her and what she was. With that realization came a fierce surge of angry pride.

"Oh, no!" She snatched her dress from the floor and held it in front of her. "I won't let you treat me like so much disposable trash. You may hold to the theory that the sins of the father fall on his family, but it isn't true. I'm a worthwhile person. I've never been in trouble with the law in my life. I know I fall short of the exalted Wickwire standards, but—"

"Will you shut up and come here!" Adam swept her into his arms with an exasperated sigh. Held closely against his hard frame, Shay felt the bold surge of his masculine response and went weak.

"Dear Lord, I want you so much." Adam's hands moved over her body with long, urgent strokes. "And you keep babbling about your father and the Wickwire standards. Are you deliberately trying to drive me out of my mind or is it an unconscious effort?"

"You don't want me," Shay refuted sadly, feeling

the tears swim in her eyes. "The only reason you brought me here tonight is to—"

Adam released her with a groan. "Sit down, Shay."

When she didn't move, he placed his hands on her shoulders and gently pushed her down onto the edge of the bed. He stood in front of her, his hands on his hips, his legs apart in an aggressive stance.

"Suppose you tell me exactly why you think I brought you here tonight, Shay."

She shifted uncomfortably on the bed. "I'd like to get dressed first," she said stiffly.

"No," Adam growled, then relented with a muttered curse. He removed his jacket, then unbuttoned his shirt. "Here." He handed it to her. "Put this on if you feel the need to cover yourself."

Shay slipped on the shirt, leaving it unbuttoned. Her fingers were shaking too much to even attempt that small task. The shirt was warm from Adam's body heat, and his musky, masculine scent clung to the soft cotton. Adam sat down beside her, so close that his trouser-clad thigh pressed against her bare one. When Shay tried to inch away, he secured his arm firmly about her waist. Her heart began to thud violently against her ribs.

"Do you really think that the reason I haven't made love to you these past days was because I didn't want you?" His voice was tinged with disbelief.

"It seemed logical to assume," Shay began, and he immediately cut her off.

"Only using the Shay Flynn Criterion of Logic. In case you failed to notice, I've spent the last two weeks knocking myself out to please you, wooing you with every bit of charm I thought I possessed." With one deft movement, he lifted her onto his lap. "Shay, the night of the blizzard, when you came home to find Bunny at the house . . ."

Shay caught her lower lip between her teeth and gnawed anxiously, not trusting herself to speak.

"I thought if I took you to bed, everything would be all right," Adam continued. "You had always been so incredibly responsive to me, so passionate and loving in bed. You weren't that night," he added ruefully.

Shay remembered the searing pain of that night, the bitterness of betrayal. "I couldn't, Adam," she whispered.

"I know, honey. That night while you slept I spent a long time analyzing our situation. Our relationship had begun in bed and I thought we'd have to backtrack and lay the groundwork that normally comes first. I wanted to win your trust and affection, I wanted to be your friend. Making sexual demands didn't seem to be the way to do it, so I vowed to back off until you gave me the sign you were ready for more." He broke off with an exaggerated sigh. "Didn't I reach you at all, Shay? Are you telling me that my noble stab at chastity was all in vain?"

Shay swallowed hard. "I—I thought you didn't want me anymore." She could hardly take it in. She felt the urgency in him, heard the hunger in his voice, and wondered if she was dreaming. "The night we went dancing, you left me to take the dog for a walk!"

"Honey, you said 'no,' remember? It nearly killed me to leave you, but I'd promised myself that I wouldn't pressure you."

His hands cupped the rounded fullness of her breasts as he nuzzled the alluring cleavage. "Didn't want you? Honey, I've been *aching* for you!" He lay back on the mattress, taking her with him, so that she lay sprawled on top of him. "What other misconceptions are you harboring in that complicated little mind of yours?"

"How do I know if they're misconceptions or truths?" Shay countered, but she was smiling into his eyes with an almost light-headed relief. She felt as if she had been sprung from a trap, and in effect Adam's words had freed her from the trap of her tormenting insecurities. She felt free, and giddy with excitement.

"I think the witness is being evasive." Adam rolled

her over, pinning her shoulders down with his weight. "Perhaps the prosecution will have to resort to more effective methods of interrogation." His mouth came down on hers with a satisfying hardness, and she parted her lips at the hot insistence of his tongue. A raging flame of desire instantly ignited her whole body into a yearning, burning conflagration.

"Oh, Adam." She sighed as she clung to him with trembling hands, arching her body into his. "I want you so much."

"Yes, I can make you want me," Adam rasped, tracing erotic little patterns on the smooth skin of her inner thigh. "But how do I make you confide in me, how can I make you believe in me? Why can you talk to Deroy and not to me, Shay? Do you know how I felt when you answered the phone at his place tonight?"

"The way I felt when I arrived home that night and found Bunny there?" Shay dared to surmise.

Adam groaned. "Worse, I think. I'd never really experienced jealousy before, Shay." He gave a small, self-mocking smile. "After all, Adam Prescott Wickwire the Third had always had and done everything a little bit better than the rest. But tonight, learning that you'd left me to go to Deroy . . . God, Shay, for the first time in my life I fully understood the term 'temporary insanity.' "

"Adam, you need never be jealous of Paul," Shay hastened to assure him.

"I'm jealous of Paul and Case and Candy and anyone else who has your trust and your confidence and . . ." He paused. "Your love. I want it, Shay. I want everything you have to give."

"But why?" she breathed, not daring to believe what her senses were telling her. "In five months—"

"—you'll give birth to my child," Adam finished in a husky voice. "And I'll bring you both home and we'll put the baby in the nursery you'll have decorated and we'll begin the task of raising our child. Together, Shay. We're staying together, and not out of some distorted sense of obligation. We'll be together because we want to be, need to be."

Was she dreaming? Did dreams come true, after all? Shay gazed into his eyes and caught her breath at what she saw there.

"I'm in love with you, Shay." Adam voiced the message his warm gray eyes had already imparted. "And I'll teach you to love and trust me if it takes a lifetime."

"Oh, Adam, I do love you!" She thought her heart would burst with joy. "So much I could die of it! But it seemed so hopeless. How could you ever love someone who had tricked you the way I did? Who was so—so very wrong for you?"

"Wrong for me? Shay, during our first weekend together last August you managed to evoke emotions in me that I never dreamed I was capable of feeling." Adam smiled down at her with a tenderness that took her breath away.

"And all the time I spend with you merely confirms that you are exactly the right woman for me. The only woman, darling. Our relationship has been deep, intense, passionate, and demanding—everything that I've never experienced with any other woman, including the confusion and the pain."

"I love you so much, Adam." The words came easily to her. She loved saying them aloud at last. "I love you and I need you." She paused to smile up at him with love-filled blue eyes. "And I do trust you, Adam. I always will."

"I'll always be there for you, Shay," he promised. He turned her in his arms, and they kissed deeply, sweetly, tumbling back on the bed together in a gentle embrace.

They clutched each other, savoring the warmth. And for a few long moments they were content to lie still, holding each other and murmuring love words as they treasured their exquisite closeness.

"I want you so much, Shay," he said hoarsely. He rose, kicked off his shoes, and quickly shed the rest of his clothes. "I'd planned to take you slowly, to make it last, but, sweetheart, I can't wait another moment for you." He settled his warm body on top of her.

"I don't want to wait." Shay lovingly stroked the fine, strong line of his jaw, and he smiled as he helped her slip off her bra and panties. "We'll take it slowly . . . next time."

"At last I've got you where I want you, right where you belong." Adam nibbled at her lips, teasing her with a string of frustrating quick little kisses that made her yearn for the hard, firm pressure of his mouth. "You're going to know tonight that you belong to me, Shay, that you are completely and everlastingly mine."

Shay wriggled sensuously beneath him, loving the feel and the taste of him. "I think I learned that lesson the first time we made love," she whispered, smoothing her hands over the hard breadth of his back and shoulders. Her fingers teased lower, to the taut curve of his buttocks, and she added, "But I want to be taught over and over again."

"A gentleman is always eager to oblige a lady." Adam began to move slowly within her, and Shay uttered a hungry little moan, losing herself in the rocketing passion that flared between them.

It was a joyously thrilling union of body and mind and spirit, forging an invincible bond of mutual ecstasy and deep love between them. Together they sailed through the rapturous seas of passion, rising higher and higher on the cresting waves until they reached the peaks and cried out their satisfaction with each other's name. They clung together as they blissfully floated to shore, bathed in the warmth of love.

They lay in each other's arms in silent, satiated repose for a long time afterward. "Adam?" Shay was the first to speak.

"Yes, love?" He cradled her against his body in a protective, possessive embrace.

"About my father . . ."

Adam cupped her chin in his hand and turned her head to his, gazing deeply in her eyes. "Shay, your father's character—or the lack of it—has no bearing whatsoever on my feelings for you. I regret your father's record because it's hurt you, but beyond that"—he shrugged—"I don't give a damn who your parents were or where you grew up or how much money your family didn't have. It's all irrelevent, Shay. I love you for what you are. You believe that now, don't you?"

Shay thought of the way he made love to her, his complete and passionate giving of himself, his tender concern for her own satisfaction. She remembered how kind he had been to her, how generous, how eager to please her. How could she not have known that he loved her? He had shown her in every way, every single day of their marriage.

Adam loved her. She luxuriated in the warmth of his arms, basking in her newly discovered love. "Yes, Adam," she said softly. "I believe you love me." Because she felt so secure with him now, she felt free to express one last, nagging doubt. "But I'm afraid your family will be a little, uh, perturbed when they hear that Dad's a crook. Your father's a *judge*, Adam!"

"Honey, my parents like you too much to hold your father against you."

"They like me?" Shay asked doubtfully.

"They told me themselves. Of course it helps that you've made their son a very happy man. Mother told me that she had never seen me so happy or so content. And Dad confided that he was relieved I hadn't married Bunny. He finds her officious. And my uncle finds her incompetent. He thoroughly approves of my marriage to you, although I'm afraid he has ulterior motives. Uncle Bill has hopes of luring your sister into the family firm."

"And you don't mind?" Shay recalled his hasty departure with Bunny when that very subject had come up.

"I don't begrudge my uncle his fantasies," he said, grinning. "But I was upset at the thought of Wickwire, Prescott & Sinclair's becoming known as a barracuda divorce firm. It wouldn't help our staid corporate image. But there's no chance of that happening, Candy assured me. She says she would be stifled in a stodgy, conservative firm."

"That sounds like Candy." She paused. "I didn't know what to think when you went off with Bunny at the party, Adam."

Adam's arms tightened possessively. "You have nothing to fear from Bunny or any other woman, Shay. In you I've found what I didn't even know had been missing from my life. Passion, love, spontaneity, and humor. We're a good match, Shay. And it's going to last between us because we're going to work to make it last."

Shay leaned up to kiss him in affirmation. Her breasts pressed softly into his chest, the nipples hard. She felt his instant response and gave him a slow, sexy smile. "You did promise that the next time would be slow and leisurely, didn't you, Adam?"

"Oh yes, baby." He lowered her back onto the mattress. "We're going to make this one last all night."

Fourteen

Five and a half months later, Adam Prescott Wickwire IV (Scotty) was delivered, following a classic late-night rush to the hospital and a relatively easy labor. Adam was by his wife's side throughout, offering aid and encouragement. They had taken natural-childbirth classes together, and the moment of their son's birth was a shared experience of love and joy, a mutual bond that would never be broken.

Adam was the first to hold his son, and he gazed down at the eight pound, blue-eyed bundle with a kind of reverential wonder.

"We're bonding," he explained to Shay as he stroked the infant's shock of dark hair. He laid a finger in the newborn's palm, and the tiny fist closed instinctively around it. Adam had taken his preparenting and infant-care classes very seriously. Little Scotty had a father—and a mother—on whom he could always depend.

Shay and Adam took their son home to a cheery yellow nursery with a large rainbow painted on one wall. A purple stuffed bear, a gift from the Art Club, sat proudly on a shelf amidst a menagerie of other stuffed animals. Shay laid the sleeping baby in his new brass crib, her heart brimming over with happiness.

Adam took her in his arms. "It's so good to have you home again," he murmured, nibbling on the curve of her neck. "Five days in the hospital is too long for you to be away from me. Maybe we'll have the next one at home."

"The next one?" Shay nipped at him playfully. "Adam Wickwire, you don't talk about having another baby to the mother of a five-day-old. Give me a little time!"

"A little time," Adam agreed with a grin. "Then we'll get to work on Brandon. The girls will come along a few years after that."

"Just how many children are you planning on having, counselor?" Shay leaned heavily against him, wrapping her arms tightly around him. She loved him so.

"As many or as few as you want, honey." He kissed her hungrily, and Shay lost herself in the magic of his love.

"I almost forgot," Adam said as he carried her to their bedroom. "We received a wedding invitation in the mail yesterday. Paulette Wilder and David Falk are getting married next month."

Shay smiled. "So Paulette finally landed her man."

Adam set her on her feet in the bedroom. "It's time for your nap," he ordered firmly. "New mothers need their rest." He helped her undress and slip into a pale lavender nightgown.

"Adam?" Her arms reached up to encircle his neck as he tucked her under the coverlet. "Would you stay with me for a while? And hold me?"

He was in bed with her two seconds later. After a long kiss, she snuggled in his arms and closed her eyes.

"I love you, Shay," Adam whispered softly. "You've made me the happiest man in the world."

"That's only fair," Shay mumbled sleepily. "Because you've made me the happiest woman."

THE EDITOR'S CORNER

For the best in summertime reading, look no further than the six superb LOVESWEPTs coming your way. As temperatures soar, what better way is there to escape from it all than by enjoying these upcoming love stories?

Barbara Boswell's newest LOVESWEPT is guaranteed to sweep you away into the marvelous world of high romance. A hell raiser from the wrong side of the tracks, Caleb Strong is back, and no red-blooded woman can blame Cheyenne Whitney Merit for giving in to his STRONG TEMPTATION, LOVESWEPT #486. The bad boy who left town years ago has grown into one virile hunk, and his hot, hungry kisses make "good girl" Cheyenne go wild with longing. But just as Caleb burns with desire for Cheyenne, so is he consumed by the need for revenge. And only her tender, healing love can drive away the darkness that threatens their fragile bond. A dramatic, thrilling story that's sensuously charged with unlimited passion.

The hero and heroine in SIZZLE by Marcia Evanick, LOVESWEPT #487, make the most unlikely couple you'll ever meet, but as Eben James and Summer Hudson find out, differences add spice to life . . . and love. Eben keeps his feet firmly planted in the ground, so when he discovers his golden-haired neighbor believes in a legendary sea monster, he's sure the gods are playing a joke on him. But there's nothing laughable about the excitement that crackles on the air whenever their gazes meet. Throwing caution to the wind, he woos Summer, and their courtship, at once uproarious and touching, will have you believing in the sheer magic of romance.

Welcome back Joan J. Domning, who presents the stormy tale of love lost, then regained, in RAINY DAY MAN, LOVESWEPT #488. Shane Halloran was trouble with a capital *T* when Merle Pierce fell hard for him in high school, but she never believed the sexy daredevil would abandon her. She devoted herself to her teenage advice column and tried to forget the man who ruined her for others. Now, more than twenty years later, fate intervenes, and Shane learns a truth Merle would have done anything to hide from him. Tempers flare but are doused in the sea of their long-suppressed passion for each other. Rest assured that all is forgiven between these two when the happy ending comes!

With her spellbinding sensuality, well-loved author Helen Mittermeyer captures A MOMENT IN TIME, LOVESWEPT #489. Hawk Dyhart acts like the consummate hero when he bravely rushes into the ocean to save a swimmer from a shark. Never mind that the shark turns out to be a diving flag and the swimmer an astonishingly beautiful woman who's furious at being rescued. Bahira Massoud is a magnificently exotic creature that Hawk must possess, but Bahira knows too well the danger of surrendering to a master of seduction. Still, she aches to taste the desire that Hawk arouses in her, and Hawk must walk a fine line to capture this sea goddess in his arms. Stunning and breathtaking, this is a romance you can't let yourself miss.

Let Victoria Leigh tantalize you with LITTLE SECRETS, LOVESWEPT #490. Ex-spy turned successful novelist I. J. Carlson drives Cassandra Lockland mad with his mocking glances and wicked come-ons. How could she be attracted to a man who provokes her each time they meet? Carlson sees the fire beneath her cool facade and stokes it with kisses that transform the love scenes in his books into sizzling reality. Once he breaches her defenses and uncovers her hidden fears, he sets out on a glorious campaign to win her trust. Will she be brave enough to face the risk of loving again? You'll be thoroughly mesmerized by this gem of a book.

Mary Kay McComas certainly lands her hero and heroine in a comedy of errors in ASKING FOR TROUBLE, LOVESWEPT #491. It all starts when Sydney Wiesman chooses Tom Ghorman from the contestants offered by the television show *Electra-Love*. He's smart, romantic, funny—the perfect man for the perfect date—but their evening together is filled with one disaster after another. Tom courageously sees them through each time trouble intervenes, but he knows this woman of his dreams can never accept the one thing in his life he can't change. Sydney must leave the safe and boring path to find the greatest adventure of all—a future with Tom. Don't miss this delectable treat.

FANFARE presents four truly spectacular books in women's popular fiction next month. Ask your bookseller for TEXAS! CHASE, the next sizzling novel in the TEXAS! trilogy by bestselling author Sandra Brown, THE MATCHMAKER by critically acclaimed Kay Hooper, RAINBOW by the very talented Patricia Potter, and FOLLOW THE SUN by ever-popular Deborah Smith.

Enjoy the summer with perfect reading from LOVESWEPT and FANFARE!

With every good wish,

Carolyn Nichols

Carolyn Nichols
Editor
LOVESWEPT
Bantam Books
666 Fifth Avenue
New York, NY 10103